G R JORDAN

Murder on the Quiet

A Highlands and Islands Detective Thriller #49

First edition

ISBN (print): 978-1-917497-37-4
ISBN (digital): 978-1-917497-36-7

This book was professionally typeset on Reedsy.
Find out more at reedsy.com

Cows are my passion. What I have ever sighed for has been to retreat to a Swiss farm, and live entirely surrounded by cows - and china.

CHARLES DICKENS

Contents

Foreword

The events of this book, while based around real and also fictitious locations around the UK, are entirely fictional and all characters do not represent any living or deceased person. All companies are fictitious representations and locations have been modified for the purposes of the story. This novel is best read looking out to the endless ocean with someone special by your side.

Acknowledgments

To Ken, Jean, Colin, Evelyn, John and Rosemary for your work in bringing this novel to completion, your time and effort is deeply appreciated.

Books by G R Jordan

The Highlands and Islands Detective series (Crime)

1. Water's Edge
2. The Bothy
3. The Horror Weekend
4. The Small Ferry
5. Dead at Third Man
6. The Pirate Club
7. A Personal Agenda
8. A Just Punishment
9. The Numerous Deaths of Santa Claus
10. Our Gated Community
11. The Satchel
12. Culhwch Alpha
13. Fair Market Value
14. The Coach Bomber
15. The Culling at Singing Sands
16. Where Justice Fails
17. The Cortado Club
18. Cleared to Die
19. Man Overboard!
20. Antisocial Behaviour
21. Rogues' Gallery
22. The Death of Macleod - Inferno Book 1

Kirsten Stewart Thrillers (Thriller)

1. A Shot at Democracy
2. The Hunted Child
3. The Express Wishes of Mr MacIver
4. The Nationalist Express
5. The Hunt for 'Red Anna'
6. The Execution of Celebrity
7. The Man Everyone Wanted
8. Busman's Holiday
9. A Personal Favour
10. Infiltrator
11. Implosion
12. Traitor

Jac Moonshine Thrillers

1. Jac's Revenge
2. Jac for the People
3. Jac the Pariah

Siobhan Duffy Mysteries

1. A Giant Killing
2. Death of the Witch
3. The Bloodied Hands
4. A Hermit's Death

The Contessa Munroe Mysteries (Cozy Mystery)

1. Corpse Reviver
2. Frostbite
3. Cobra's Fang

The Patrick Smythe Series (Crime)

1. The Disappearance of Russell Hadleigh
2. The Graves of Calgary Bay
3. The Fairy Pools Gathering

Austerley & Kirkgordon Series (Fantasy)

1. Crescendo!
2. The Darkness at Dillingham
3. Dagon's Revenge
4. Ship of Doom

Supernatural and Elder Threat Assessment Agency (SETAA) Series (Fantasy)

1. Scarlett O'Meara: Beastmaster

Island Adventures Series (Cosy Fantasy Adventure)

1. Surface Tensions

Dark Wen Series (Horror Fantasy)

1. The Blasphemous Welcome
2. The Demon's Chalice

Chapter 01

The man stumbled along with the crash of the waves echoing in his ears. It was windy tonight, but then out here it was often windy. A brutal piece of rock, standing so far away from the mainland, even from the Hebrides, miles off the west coast of Scotland. And here they built a paradise, or at least, they were building one.

He could hear their footsteps behind. There were torches, people muttering curses aimed at him. But he wasn't the bad one here. He wasn't the one who would do anything that needed to be forgiven. He was just a worker who knew too much.

For all that it was windy, there was no cloud cover. He could see the pontoon in the distance. They were building luxury pods, which were beautiful during the day. He had seen out of them the view across the endless sea, the brainchild of people with far too much money. How did you get away from people? How did you get to a place that was so remote and yet bring all that you needed with you?

Of course, all that you needed wasn't just food and shelter. Not even comfort. There was a shooting range out here. Why? And it was crass enough to be built close to bird colonies. That was madness in itself, but then these type of people, the people with the money for this, they weren't worried about anything else. You didn't make that sort of money by caring about other people.

But he'd taken the job, and he'd taken their money. His specialism as a plumber had been put to good use, for there were pipes everywhere; the heating systems to maintain, waste disposal, water to all the amenities. And there were amenities here, built on what had been wild, truly wild. So far away! A place, he thought, that should have stayed belonging to the birds. Birds can't sign contracts, can they? Birds can't argue in court for their rights to stay, and they own nothing. They dropped their poo on the workers from above, but that was the only defence they had. He would need a defence now.

He would need to get off of here. But how? He thought about calling, raising the problem to the outside world. But they'd taken down the satellite link. It was gone. He had no way of contacting anyone else. They'd also covered the boat by posting men on board. Otherwise, he could have made a run for it—got in the boat and gone.

The other workboats would be here soon too. And that's why they came for him. That's why they were hunting him down. Because they knew he knew something. And they needed to find out just what. But if they did, he was a dead man. For what he knew would get them all locked away.

The voices came stronger now from behind, and he dropped onto the pontoon. There wasn't really anywhere else to go here. He could jump into one of the pods, but suddenly he had a better idea.

He slipped into the water, feeling the freezing cold drive up through his body, and slipped down under the pontoon, taking a large breath. They wouldn't be able to see into the water, not in this light. He wondered how long he could hold his breath. He counted, but he did not know if he was accurate. What it did was keep the panic away. That's what they said, wasn't it? Don't concentrate on the fear. Don't concentrate on everything that's coming at you and telling you to panic. Concentrate on something simple. A job. He needed to count. And now he did.

Being under the water, he couldn't tell where they were. When he surfaced, he'd try to surface underneath a pontoon. Slowly. Take another breath if he had to.

His hands reached up, touching the side of the float, feeling across, until he found a gap in the middle of the pontoon. He could surface there, for the floats ran around the edge. Let himself float until he broke the water with his head. He refrained from taking an almighty gasp and tried to breathe in steadily, the water falling off his ears. Struggling at first to hear clearly, he suddenly made out the sound of footsteps going across the pontoon. They made him grab another breath and sink back down.

He needed to get the documentation. They'd written it down. They'd written the names; all he had to do was find it. It was hidden in his pod. One of a few temporary pods they were using out here. They weren't like the stunning accommodation that would be the permanent fixture. These were small pods on floats that they'd made up. He shared it with two other people, but he'd stowed the documentation away.

He would need to get it to the mainland. Need to get it to someone. It would explain. Explain how they were going to do it. But that was the thing. They'd had to think about it as they were building the structure. There'd been some minor difficulties. Maybe when they'd made the original plans, away in some office or some hideout somewhere, they'd sat down and said, 'This is how we were going to do it.' But now in situ after building the facility. There'd been issues. So, they had to rethink exactly how it worked.

The difficulty with such a scheme as this was that it was complex enough to put it onto paper, at least for everyone to check, everyone to look at it. And he had taken that paper by accident. He'd wandered into one of the offices looking for his boss. The man hadn't been there, but neither had anyone else. He was sure the door was meant to have been locked.

Or were they just sure that no one would go there? It was, after all, the place they'd said not to go to. But he'd gone in. As he stood looking around, it had caught his eye, and he'd read the documentation. He'd read the plans, and then he'd grabbed them and was gone. In his horror, he'd taken it, thinking he could show his boss. After he'd gone with the plans, everything had changed. They must have seen him at the facility, because suddenly, people were talking to him.

He'd hidden it among his gear, and then shifted it to the temporary pod. But now, he'd need it again. He'd watched them from a distance search the pod, and they'd found nothing. But then again, they hadn't looked inside the pipe. He needed to get it back because he couldn't bring people here; these were temporary pods and the documentation would be destroyed, as these pods would be, in a few weeks' time. No, he needed to get the documentation to the mainland.

Slowly, he lifted his head through the water underneath the pontoon. He could hear nothing. He waited a bit longer in case his ears were deceiving him. But he was okay. He was fine. Carefully, he pulled himself up onto the pontoon, staying lying down and flat on his belly. He couldn't hear anything. And so he stood up gingerly.

One thing that struck him was why they didn't just take care of this in the courts. Their plans, their ideas for murder could have been achieved, surely, in the courts. It could have been achieved with the money they had. In truth, the man didn't understand the full scheme of things, only the horror that had been written out in front of him. And slowly, he crept along the pontoon, round the side of one of the extensive gaps between the new pods, the luxury ones that were being built.

He was able to half lower himself into the water, but his teeth were chattering. He fought hard to stop them and worked along the side, half in the water, half out, until he reached a point where he could swim towards his own temporary pod. All the temporary pods were connected by pontoons. But maybe there'd be somebody at the front of one of them. So he swam as quietly as he could to the edge of his own pod. There was no one about. But of course, that's because they were all out there looking for him. They'd already searched the pods. There was nothing here.

Now, carefully, he pulled himself up onto the pontoon. Other workers would be asleep. And he thought about crying out, waking them. But he'd have to be so quick in explaining. And then what? Two factions trapped on a place like this? Nowhere to go?

No, better if he could just sneak off. He'd be putting too many others at risk.

Carefully, he approached the door of his pod, opening it and looking quickly inside. There was no one there. So, he closed the door and switched on the light. So far out from the mainland, you got no true mobile signal. And any internet access you had was controlled by the company through its satellite connection. It had gone down, strangely enough. Anyway, the phone had been in the room, and they'd have taken it by now.

Approaching the corner of the room, he leant down underneath the sink. Towards the back was a piece of pipe that didn't connect to anywhere. It looked like it might, for it seemed to feed from outside. But it was actually a redundant piece of pipe on this pod.

And as he unscrewed it, he pulled out the documentation from the middle of it, all curled up neatly. He took it, held it in his hand, trying not to get it too wet. Replacing the pipe back, he switched off the light of the pod. Stepping back onto the pontoon, he could hear voices. They were coming towards the pods now, the employee ones. There was only one pontoon leading back to the primary installation. He slipped back into the water, holding the documentation in his teeth to keep it from being soaked.

Slowly he swam, head above water. He wanted to submerge, to get away without being seen. Where could he go? How long did he wait? His best bet would surely be to hide up on the island and then try to take over the fast boat when it came with supplies. They came daily. On the other hand, he could, of course, call the Coastguard from it, radio in a Mayday. This was his genuine hope—for other people to come, and for him to stay hidden.

As he swam along, he could hear them now on the pontoon towards his own pod. But he couldn't stay in the water for too long either. It was freezing cold. You were way out here, maybe a hundred miles off the west coast of Scotland. He needed to get out of the water and to get somewhere safe.

Ahead of him was a pod that would be part of the main fixture. It was half complete, but the front of it was still wide open, for they hadn't brought the glass yet to seal the revolving canopy. It would eventually have an almost shell-like look, where the front would lift back, and it could be exposed to whatever weather was out there, and also the view, obviously only on the nicer days. But, for now, it was an open cabin with the bare basics inside.

Slowly, he clambered out of the water and into the pod. He knew the design from when he'd worked on them and had already done some of the pipework underneath the main floor. He looked at the floor panelling. *Yes*, he thought. *That was the place to put it.*

He went to the panel on the far side and, being the plumber that he was, pulled a screwdriver out of his back pocket. The panel was watertight, and when he pulled it up, there were several pipes passing through where the panel was as well as a couple of valves. He took the documentation and slipped it in behind. It would be dry and safe there. Better than him carrying it. After all. It'd be too easy for it to get destroyed, with the rain outside.

No, he would hide it here, and then he'd try to get to the shooting range, get shelter for the night, and then maybe swim for St Kilda. Was that a possibility? Or even get a small raft or boat to get over there. St Kilda, after all, had a place to communicate from. There were people who still worked there, and who weren't from the company.

He placed the panel back on top, and screwed it back in when he heard the sound. Carefully, he turned with the screwdriver, edging towards the door. The panel wasn't completely screwed back in, only half of it, but he was worried. Were they here?

The screwdriver would be a good defence. No, it wasn't a knife, it wasn't a gun, but you could attack with it. You could go at someone with it.

Carefully, he slid across the room, although in truth he squelched, to some degree. He stood waiting, to see if the door would open. It seemed like an age. and he could hear somebody outside the pod, but then he realised that some of that movement was from inside. He turned sharply, panicking that someone was behind him, only to find that they were indeed. The blow struck him across the head, and everything went black.

Chapter 02

Hope McGrath turned on the shower and stuck her hand underneath. The water came out bitterly cold, and she gave a yelp, but then jumped in anyway, letting the water splash across her back at first. Soon the heat engaged, and she stood letting the water flow over her.

She was beaming, smiling to nobody as she stood there, washing her red hair, pulling the long strands out behind her. Hope looked down at her body, the lower half having changed, knowing that she was now a different woman to the one who'd been there six months before. She had the scars of childbirth, but she was so happy with herself, so happy with her little family. They'd be in the next room, where John had taken Ian through and was probably holding him, cuddling him away on the sofa.

It had been several months now since she'd given birth in rather dramatic fashion, but she didn't care about that now. For her wee one, Ian, was all right, and her partner, John, had offered her the chance to go back and be the detective she was before. She'd made mistakes in her life with men, been with those who would try to dominate her, but John, John was all about her. She wanted to be all about him, too. In truth, the pair of them were exhausted, but also incredibly happy. She was in the shower for some ten minutes before she heard a knock at the door.

When she climbed out of the shower, she could hear voices in the other room. She dried herself quickly, went to throw on a T-shirt and pants, but John then stepped into the bedroom.

'Seoras is here,' he said, and stood looking at her. She simply grinned back. 'I'm not sure that's going to be the most appropriate thing to wear in front of him,' he said.

Hope stepped forward, threw her arms around John, and whispered in his ear, 'Do you trust him with our kid?'

John laughed as she ran her hand down his back, but he said in her ear, 'I'm not sure that his ability would match up to his promise.'

Hope laughed. 'True,' she said. 'I'll be through in a minute. I'll just throw on something a little less revealing.'

John kissed her, and disappeared back into the room. Then, after Hope pulled on a pair of jeans and a baggy jumper, she bounded out through into the living room. DCI Seoras Macleod sat in an armchair with her young son cradled in his arms.

'You just can't wait to come round here, can you? Can we get an evening or two?' She laughed.

Macleod looked up. 'Jane says I have to take payment for this. Now that I'm retiring, we need an income.'

'You can have a cup of coffee,' said Hope, almost skipping her way into the kitchen.

'John says you've got some good news.'

'Well, it depends on how you look at it. Good news for us.'

'Oh,' said Macleod. 'How do you mean?'

Hope ignored him for a moment, throwing the beans into

the grinder and then filling up the machine. Once she'd poured in the water and got it going, she turned back to Macleod.

'John's gone and won us a holiday.'

'A holiday?' said Macleod.

'Yes,' said Hope. 'It's just that it's meant to be the two weeks after I come back. I want to extend the maternity leave for a couple of weeks.'

'All right,' said Macleod.

'I know you want to be going. I know you want to do a month's handover to me. You want to stay about for a bit and then you want to go,' said Hope. 'But this isn't just like a holiday. It's not like we've got a couple of weeks in Benidorm.'

'Well, where is it then?'

'It's on Boreray,' said John.

'Where?' asked Macleod.

'It's one of the islands in the St Kilda archipelago. It's the place they're building out there.' Macleod looked blank. 'Do you not listen to anything?'

'Was it on the news?' asked Macleod.

'It's been on the news. It's been all over social media. It's been—'

She saw Macleod looking at her. 'Well, you wouldn't have seen it on social media, but you might have caught it in the news.'

'Don't watch the news much,' said Macleod, 'especially if I'm on it. Jane said I did all right with the press when you were away.'

'She's just saying that,' said Hope. 'Now you're leaving, I can tell you how rubbish you are.' He glared at her, and she burst out laughing. She really was buzzing today. Just buzzing.

'Is this wee one ready to go on holiday?' asked Macleod.

'He's doing great, isn't he? He's just doing so well,' said Hope.

'What is it then?' asked Macleod. 'If it's not sun and sand.'

'It's a holiday of a lifetime,' said Hope. 'They've built out at Boreray, an island getaway. It's meant to be like the Maldives.'

'It's over at St Kilda,' said Macleod. 'How is it like the Maldives?'

'Well, they've got these little pods that you live in.'

'Okay,' said Macleod, 'but I ask again. How is it like the Maldives? Jane wanted to go to the Maldives. Jane wants me to sit in a hut in the middle of the sea. What's the point of that?'

'Relaxation, space, quiet, time for the two of you to connect,' said Hope. 'She probably wants more time with you. Get up to all that stuff you don't want to talk about in the office.'

'What stuff?' started Macleod and then stopped. Hope thought he looked slightly embarrassed. Seoras never talked about things like that. When he talked about Jane, and if he was talking about intimacy, it was still very formal. He never broke cover, not truly. Probably with Jane. It was a side of him that even Hope didn't get to see that much of.

'They've got a rifle range. They've got canoeing, kayaks, all sorts of things. You can go scuba diving, everything out there. And they've got an amazing kitchen. And basically, nobody was going to get to go out there except people with serious money,' said Hope.

'So what? They've built a playground for the rich, and you're off to it,' said Macleod.

'Don't put it like that. And yes, we are. Yes, they did. They've built it for themselves, and very rich people were going to get involved. But they did a draw for charity, and John's gone and won it.'

Hope smiled over at John, who was beaming too.

'We were wondering, Seoras,' said John, 'seriously. I know it's an inconvenience. I know it's not what you want. Maybe not what Jane wants, but do you think you could do an extra two weeks? I mean, maybe you could shorten the handover.'

'And this is costing you guys anything?' said Macleod.

'No,' said Hope. 'It's all inclusive. You go away, and there's no contact with the outside world. I mean, it's a chance for the three of us just to be completely away. It's been great here in my time off,' said Hope. 'But this, this would give John a chance to do things, things he hasn't been able to do here. We've had months of just being busy. It's been wonderful, but so busy. Going out there, we can just collapse. We can just—'

'I get it,' said Macleod. 'I get it.'

'I don't think you do,' said Hope. 'They have these pods that you sleep in.' Macleod raised an eyebrow. 'When I say pod, I mean, it's an unbelievable room. But they call it a pod because it's sitting there on the sea. You've got the island beside you. They have these pods, according to the pictures anyway, and this pontoon that goes out to your pod. And your pod's got everything in it, an en-suite, all of that. The front of the pod's this giant window. It scrolls up so you can be there with all that fresh air around your room, with all of that—'

Macleod was looking at her questioningly. 'So, you're saying to me you're going to the west coast of Scotland and a hundred and odd miles beyond and you're going to live in a room with a big open window. I'd have thought you'd have wanted the most thermally insulated building ever.'

'What are you like?' said Hope suddenly. 'This is a chance to be out in the wild, a chance to be somewhere that nobody else will ever be. This is—'

'And you're on the sea,' said Macleod.

'Yes, you're right there on the sea. Imagine it, John and I lying there together, the wee man between us. Just staring out with the fresh sea air wafting around you as you lie in bed waking up.'

Macleod was still looking at her as if she'd lost her head. 'And the sea laps up all the way? You keep hearing the sea all night?' asked Macleod. 'Yes,' said Hope, 'I mean it's romantic, it's inspirational, it's being out there in the wild, it's—'

'I would need the toilet. I have difficulty enough through the night,' said Macleod. 'But to hear the sea, all the time, lapping up. Good job there's an en suite.'

Hope stared at him and burst out laughing. 'You are unreal. If Jane heard you say that she would go through you.'

'Jane is very well aware of my issues as I get older in life. And I am very well aware of hers. We do not need to go to places that provide running water beside you at night. We need to go to places with good en suite facilities where they make you nice food and they're able to pick you up and take you places.'

'So what, you're going on a coach tour?'

'Going away, when I retire. We've been looking at the finances,' said Macleod. 'Jane wants to travel. Jane wants to see things. We will be based, obviously, at our house, but we'll be going away more than we ever did. With my work, she's never had that opportunity. We went on that cruise and . . .'

'You went on that cruise and found dead bodies,' said Hope. 'You need to go on something where you don't find bodies.'

'I didn't pick it. It wasn't advertised in the sense of, "Hey, come and have a busman's holiday."'

'No, but I bet you went in hook, line, and sinker when it happened. I bet you were on the case.

Macleod looked serious now. 'People died. It was my duty.'

'And it won't be soon. Soon you'll just be Mr Macleod.'

'No,' he said. 'No, I've been thinking about this. I was always DS Macleod. DC Macleod. DCI Macleod. I was always Macleod. Even when they changed the force to get us to use first names, you did it, but you're not old-school. Most of the old-school still wanted to call me "Sir". Or Macleod at least. I'm going to be Seoras. And that's what this wee guy's going to know me as,' said Macleod, cuddling Ian tightly. 'I'm going to be Seoras.'

'Uncle Seoras,' said Hope, 'Uncle Seoras and Auntie Jane.'

Macleod looked over and smiled. 'I like that.'

'Well, he hasn't got any aunts and uncles,' said Hope, 'it's just me, and it's just John. We haven't got any brothers or sisters, so, no aunts or uncles, so you can be aunt and uncle.'

Macleod smiled as Hope turned back to the kitchen to get the coffee. She placed one down beside Macleod on the table, telling him to be careful around the wee one.

'How's everyone taken to the announcement?' asked John.

'We've got a few things in the offing,' said Macleod. 'Hope will be more aware of this maybe than you, John, but Perry and Susan got very close, as did Tanya. But Perry's now an item with Tanya. Susan came to me and talked about whether she should work with Perry now. They seem okay, they seem to get on, but, well, I think she's finding it tough.'

'She thinks she blew that one,' said Hope. 'She did. She definitely blew it. Perry's a good guy. But you can't keep a good guy waiting forever.'

'And Tanya's a good woman for him,' said Macleod. 'We may have some other things on the horizon.'

'Such as?' asked Hope.

'Sabine came to me the other day. I think, well, I think she and Emmett are—'

'You think they're close,' said Hope.

'I'm just glad I grabbed you when I did,' said John. And Macleod almost laughed at that.

'What are you saying then?' asked Hope.

'Well, I don't know. I could probably get involved now,' said Macleod. 'I don't really want to touch Clarissa with Patterson. He's good for her. Superb. You've got Ross at the moment. Sabine, well, Sabine's sergeant level. Ross is also, but you know he hasn't been totally happy with the sergeant role.'

'You want to shift Ross? Give me Sabine. What's happening with Susan?'

'I think if Sabine becomes an item with Emmett,' said Macleod, 'they need to split work-wise. They can't be on the same team. Susan wants to move. That would be a straight swap. Except you'd have an extra sergeant, and he wouldn't. I'm not worried about Emmett. He just needs somebody with him. Sabine happened to be a sergeant, and they looked like a good fit. Emmett's different to work with.

'But Susan would be capable. She also fits the profile. Emmett's not somebody to handle the big guys. Susan's a live wire, like yourself.'

'Well, that's quite a compliment,' said Hope.

'You always were. You did a lot of the legwork when I couldn't,' said Macleod. 'Perry's not like that either. So, if you take Susan out of your team, you're going to need somebody who can handle that side. But you'd have two sergeants. How does that work? What place does Ross take? Is he going to step up and be your sidekick? I can put the wheels in motion. But I need to know what you want. Once I'm gone, in comes another DCI. They may have other ideas. They may not be as amenable as I am.'

Hope knew what he meant. And Macleod, for all that everybody thought him to be serious and determined, listened to her.

'But don't let it ruin your holiday,' said Macleod. 'You go away and have a wonderful break. I'll organise the extra two weeks. I'm sure Jane will go for it. Especially with you getting time away with this little man. But once I'm out, I'm out. And I can't influence things.

'So if you want things to happen before that, and get put in motion, I need to know. You need to take care of the family,' he said. 'I'm not there to do it anymore. Whoever moves into my place, you're going to have to work them, control them.'

'Either that or set Clarissa on them,' retorted Hope.

Macleod looked, and then he laughed. 'Not my problem anymore,' he said. 'Not my problem.'

Chapter 03

It was a crisp November morning as the plane touched down on Stornoway's large runway. It was wide for the ATR42, which stopped short of the intersection and taxied in onto the main apron. Hope was sitting with Ian on her lap, the little belt around the baby, and she couldn't help but smile. The child had just deposited into his nappy about two minutes before they landed, and Hope would have to disappear to change him. It was that or she got the cases while John did it.

She felt that during this holiday she should do the domestics as John was letting her go back to work in a couple of weeks. Then he would no doubt deal with more poo than she could ever imagine.

They were met at the airport by a taxi, which took them down to Stornoway Harbour. There was a large cruiser sitting waiting for them, with many other guests who'd arrived before them already on board. Their bags were taken, and Hope and John stepped onto the boat, little Ian in a baby sling, carried by Hope.

'Look at this,' said Hope.

'Have you ever been on a boat like this?' asked John.

'Not recreationally,' said Hope, and smiled back.

She was offered champagne, but given she was breastfeeding, she took an orange juice and sat down with John for the cruise out. There must have been around twenty guests on board, at least, and most seemed to talk to each other. In truth, Hope and John seemed to be on their own. No one coming ventured to talk to them, but Hope didn't care.

This was a time for quiet, in a way, for her family. This was a time for John, little Ian, and her to be close again. Just spend time without having to think before she went back to the day job. In the upcoming months, she would work hard. John would work hard at home. Ian would grow and life would be full on again. This was a time to be pampered. She would not force herself to talk to other people. If they wanted to talk to her, that would be fine. Her focus was on John and Ian.

The sea is rough enough, thought Hope. John certainly seemed to be bothered more by it than she was. Her red hair wasn't in a ponytail, but blowing in the wind, which made her think she should put it into one. But John liked it out when they were together.

He said the ponytail meant work. Her hair out meant it was time for him and family. And it was true. It was funny how the little things sometimes showed the mould you were in. She hadn't worn her hair in a ponytail for several weeks now. She liked it out, and occasionally little Ian would reach up and grab it, pulling at her hair. It was cute, and he didn't have the strength to do any damage.

She stared out at the sea, thinking about what Macleod had said. What would her team be when she got back? How would she organise them? She guessed she was going to get more involved in decisions like this. And Macleod had said she'd have to look after the family. It felt like a family, but not this little family. Not this special family. She felt Macleod was becoming part of that special family, though. Uncle Seoras and Auntie Jane. She was happy for him. He'd been such an arse when they first met.

No, he hadn't, she thought. *He was damaged. Incredibly damaged. People wouldn't have seen it. Many would have written him off as a particular type of person. Seoras was warm. Caring. A brutally efficient detective. He could read people. He could see what was going on in their heads, much more than she could. But they'd been a good team. Now she'd have to build the team.*

And she thought about Ross. She still didn't see Ross and her as a team. He'd been part of the team but it had always been Macleod and her. Could it be Ross and her? Did he have the drive for it? She didn't need to think about that now. She wasn't keen on losing Susan though. Susan was like her. They got on well, but maybe she needed to lose her. Susan didn't need to be a clone of Hope. She needed to be Susan. Emmett would certainly be different for her. Hope liked Emmett. Well, he was strange. And Sabine coming in? She was professional but was she too much like Hope?

'You might not have your hair in a ponytail, but you are thinking about work. Now that stops,' said John.

'Sorry,' said Hope. 'Has anybody said hello?'

'I don't think they're really that appreciative of our being here. But I couldn't give a stuff,' said John. 'We're here and we're going to enjoy this. And if we spend all two weeks in our pod, I couldn't care less.'

'No, we'll do a bit more than that,' said Hope. 'I fancy doing a bit of kayaking. A bit of swimming out there.'

'I'll be freezing,' said John.

'Do you think they'd get annoyed if we opened the pod up in the morning and did a quick skinny dip before getting back in?'

'You're outrageous,' said John.

'I remember doing it before. Not from a pod in these waters. When I was younger. Backpacking across Europe. We got up one morning, the ones I was with, and went skinny dipping. Of course, I had my figure back then,' said Hope.

'You still have your figure,' said John.

'It's not the same though, is it?'

She noticed he was staring at her, almost angrily. 'You don't say that because it's not true,' said John. 'I think I might love it even more.'

'Don't be daft,' said Hope. 'It's shifted. I don't have the same—'

'You're a mum,' he said. 'It's quite special. It may even be more of a turn-on.'

Hope looked around her. 'Not out loud.'

'Why not?' said John. 'What do they care? They will not care about you. They're not going to care about my sexy wife.'

Hope laughed. John sat down with his arm around her as she held on to little Ian. 'Let's just make sure we have a good time,' said Hope.

It took several hours before the boat arrived at the St Kilda archipelago. They could see Hirta, the larger of the islands, sticking out from the vast sea around them. But the boat veered away over to Boreray, and Hope's breath was taken away by what she saw. At one point, there would have been a large, sheer rock island there. But now attached to it there were several large pods. Like they'd been taken off a moon basin, plonked down at the sea. It really was quite space-age.

She thought back to those 60s programmes, or was it the early 70s, that she'd seen on the repeat . Part of her wanted to get dressed up in the purple hair and silver costumes, because she felt they fitted this strange sea base they were arriving at. The pods were on the outside looking out to sea, connected to the primary structure by a pontoon. From the pods, you had an undisturbed view of the sea and the ocean before you.

'Look at that,' said Hope. 'That's where we're going to be.'

'There's stuff up on the island too,' said John.

They were standing now, watching as the boat came in to dock at the rear side of the facility, away from the pods. Hope noticed there weren't many on the pontoon that the boat arrived at. She counted five. One of them smiled broadly and seemed in charge.

'I'm Hamish. All come aboard, please. All come aboard. We'll take you through to the main common room and then show you to your pods. We'll do a tour in about an hour so you can see all that this wonderful facility offers. But welcome. Welcome out to Boreray. They want to call it the Northern Maldives, but let's face it, it's much better than that.'

Hope tried to watch as cases were offloaded but she was guided through, along with John, into a large common room. She sat down until eventually Hamish came to them, last of the group, to be shown to their pod.

'You're one of the competition winners,' said Hamish. 'Well, my name's Hamish, and I'm here to make sure that your stay is as wonderful as possible. We'll show you through to the pod, first of all. You can rest, get changed if you wish. You're welcome to wear what you want round here, or not what you want.'

'What do you mean by that?' asked Hope, half laughing.

'This is a place for those who want to get away,' said Hamish. 'Congratulations on winning the chance to experience what it's like for those with more money than possibly sense,' and gave a laugh. 'But don't let them hear me telling you that.'

'So what? Do some of them like . . . not wear anything?' asked John.

Hamish laughed. 'If they wanted not to, they're welcome to walk around in whatever. But no, I don't think we'll be seeing a type of nudist colony. To be honest, in November, it might not be the weather for it outside. This way,' said Hamish, laughing.

He was quite a stocky man, possibly in his early fifties, but he looked strong. His arms were muscular, and he had tight curls on his head. His beard too gave him the look of a sea captain. Although his accent was difficult to place. Hamish walked them down an outside pontoon that led down to their pod. There, he told Hope to put her hand onto a scanner. He then got John to do the same. The next time Hope touched it, a door slid open into their pod. Hamish stepped inside.

'Welcome to what I think is quite unique. You'll see that through the window you have got an uninterrupted sea. At the front here, there are some small railings and steps down into the sea if you wish to go for a swim. You can take life jackets from us, buoyancy aids, and you can tie yourself to the pod, in case you're worried about disappearing off in the tide. It can be quite strong in certain parts. I don't know if either of you are a good swimmer.'

'I swim,' said Hope. 'I swim well.'

'Well, enjoy it,' said Hamish. 'Double bed for you. This is one of the most comfortable beds you'll ever sleep in. I guarantee you that. We've got a very minimal cover on the bed because you can set the temperature in the room to suit yourselves. No one will look in through this window unless somebody comes past in a boat, and to be honest, we're quite far out for that. So, feel free to be however you want to be in this room. Cot beside the bed in case you need it. Through here is your en suite,' he said, pressing a button, and the door slid back.

Hope followed him through. There was a large shower, but there was also a jacuzzi bath, big enough for at least three to four people.

'Use as you will. All of your toiletries are inside the cupboards. You need anything else, call me. There's wardrobe space in here,' said Hamish, stepping out back into the pod and then pressing another button. When a door opened, Hope walked into a wardrobe that was big enough to swing a cat in.

'It's amazing,' said Hope. 'It's truly amazing.'

'We'll be doing a tour in an hour, but in case you want to get changed, freshened up, whatever, I'll just leave you be. Be back in an hour's time, up into the main lounge. We'll do a tour, and then after that, the two weeks are yours to do as you wish. You'll find there are no restrictions here. You do as you please. Obviously, we've got other guests, so please, we try to get on together. Other than that, there's a button in the pod if you need anything. Or you'll see us about. There aren't many staff. That's deliberate. This is your time away, your private space.' Hamish almost skipped by before leaving the pod.

'Wow,' said Hope. She could feel John sliding his arms around her shoulders, pulling her close from behind.

'Perfect,' he said. 'We've got an hour. What do you want to do? Is he asleep?' asked John.

'I think so.'

'Let's freshen up then.'

Hope picked up Ian and set him down in the cot. There was

a small blanket which she put across him. 'You think he's going to be okay in there?'

'He's fine. You'll soon hear him if he shouts.'

Hope looked around. She popped forward to the window, noticing a panel beside it. She tapped one button, and the window lifted, sliding back along its frame, rolling back like the sunroof in a car. The wind wasn't very strong but the breeze was enough to be felt as it caressed her body. Then she felt arms around her.

'I'm going to want to swim out there,' she said.

'Well, if you want to relive your youth, you can jump in that water. I, for one, am not getting in it without a wetsuit,' said John. 'It's freezing.'

'So you're telling me if I jumped in there starkers, you wouldn't follow?'

'Absolutely not,' said John. 'I might watch, though.'

She slapped his thigh. As he pulled her close and kissed her neck, she pressed the button, and the window slid back down, securing the pod again.

'Fancy a shower?' she asked.

'Yes,' said John. 'Absolutely. You going first?'

'He's asleep,' said Hope. 'He's asleep, and that's a big shower.' She kissed him on the cheek, and by the time she'd reached the door to the bathroom, all of her clothes were lying on the floor.

Inside the shower, they cuddled tight, just enjoying the moment with each other. As they did so, Hope thought she could hear the next pod. The pods weren't far away from each other, and out here in the bathroom, she was maybe closer to the edge of the other one.

'It's not like they'll find you here.'

'Did you hear that?' asked Hope. 'What does that mean? What are they saying? Who says that?'

John pulled her close. 'Switch off,' he said.

'Switch off?'

'I don't want the detective. I want my woman here.'

'Your woman's always here,' said Hope. 'He said an hour before the tour, didn't he?'

'More like 55 minutes now.'

'I hope we've got enough water,' said Hope.

Chapter 04

Hope pulled a t-shirt over her head before pulling the shorts on. It would be cold and blustery outside, but she didn't care. She could always grab a jacket. After all, she doubted they would take them too far away from the main building. John had moved into a pair of jogging bottoms and a t-shirt as well, and Hope pulled the baby carrier for Ian onto her shoulders.

'I'll take him if you want,' said John.

'No,' said Hope. 'I will not get to carry him during the day in a couple of weeks. You'll have him all the time. I want him here. I want him close.'

She placed Ian inside the baby carrier, and he snuggled up tight to her chest.

'Sometimes I get jealous of him,' said John.

'Good,' said Hope, laughing. 'Come on. He said, an hour. We'll be late.'

'We are not late. We are a couple of minutes early. And do you think anybody else in these other pods is going to give a stuff whether they arrive on time for us?'

'That's not the point,' said Hope. 'It's who we are. Come on.'

They exited the pod holding hands as they walked along

the pontoon to the main lounge area they had originally been taken to. Hamish was there and told them to grab a drink. On the side were champagne, whisky, and many alcoholic drinks, as well as fresh orange juice and other exotic fruits.

Hope took an orange juice while John grabbed himself a beer. They sat down on what were incredibly comfortable chairs and waited for others to arrive. John had been correct; most of the others couldn't care less about being on time. And it was a good twenty minutes after the hour before Hamish could start his little talk. He stood almost surrounded in a semicircle as everyone else sat in chairs, some paying attention, some not.

'Welcome,' said Hamish. 'I would say welcome to whatever this place is going to be called, but really that's up to most of you, since you were the ones who paid for it. I'm Hamish, and I'm here to make your day as pleasant as possible, but by design, this is your home. You have John and Hope with you, who'll be sharing it over the next two weeks, along with little Ian, and I know they're very excited about being here.'

Hope noted that few other guests said hello, but a young woman nodded over towards her.

'I'll take you on a tour. Remember, everywhere here is yours to walk around, to see, obviously other than your own pods. There's one area at the back, which is the staff quarters, and I would ask that you treat that the same way as you treat your own pod. That's our space when we're not needed in our downtime. But we are here for you. So, if you need us, you can ring the bell at any point.

'First, let's introduce the staff. I'm Hamish, the resort's manager. You're here to relax, but it is self-catering. We're not here to feed you unless you want fed. If you need fed, we have Ollie. He's our professional chef. Ollie is a Michelin star chef, and he's quite happy to help teach cookery as well as provide your dinner. He has a wide-ranging, well-stocked larder, which you're welcome to walk in and use anything of as it is yours. Tell Ollie what you want for your dinner, and he'll make it, but you are more than welcome to make it yourself. Explore. If you need help to make it, if you're not sure about how to, Ollie will happily cook it with you.'

'We have two activity directors. As we go around on the tour, you'll see what we offer, and Helena and Christophe are here for your safety but also to help you with any of the activities. They're more than trained in each of the disciplines that you'll require, including our shooting range over on the far side of Boreray. But we'll get to that in a minute. We also have two cleaners here, Ella and Geordie.'

Two young people stepped out from behind the scenes and gave a little bow. They had shorts and t-shirts on, but they were uniform based, and Hope thought they looked rather well built for people here to do cleaning jobs. They were in their early twenties and smiled as they were introduced.

'There's a stocked bar. We also have beer on tap. You're quite welcome to come along and take whatever you want. This is the main lounge that you're in at the moment. Usable by everyone. We have some smaller lounges off this, and we ask that when someone is in there and has requested quiet, that you don't go in. There are three or four of those. It should be plenty for us to share around.

'You can dine in those if you want to dine on your own, or you can dine in here. If you don't wish to do your dishes, leave them. Ellen and Geordie will sort them out. After all, this is your break, your holiday. We have an extensive library as well,' he said, pointing to a door at the rear of the main lounge. 'We also have a small cinema with a large stock of films, including some of the most recent ones. This area, at the rear of the lounge, is where you can make your cappuccinos or whatever type of coffee, teas, whatever you want. If you need them made for you, just call. Ollie or Ella or Geordie will be more than happy. They're all trained baristas.

'We get a fresh supply of fruit every three days, as well as other foodstuffs. We are, however, completely on our own here. There is no Wi-Fi access, no mobile phone signal. That is how you asked for it when you built the place. There is only one radio out and one satellite phone. It's in the workers' quarters at the back, in a small room, and that's purely in case of any emergencies. We are within flying time of a hospital. There is also a rescue helicopter based in Stornoway that can come to our aid. I am medically trained, though, if you have any minor issues that you wish dealt with. You can talk to me, or we can come through and talk on the phone to doctors online, or we can get you flown off as needs be. Let's hope it doesn't come to that.

'If you go through the door on the far side,' said Hamish, 'that'll take you out to some jetties. There are kayaks, we've also got canoes at our small harbour-type base. There are rowboats available as well. We don't have any powered boats. We have some jet skis. However, their range isn't great, and they can go through fuel, so the furthest you will travel on them in a day is fifty miles. So don't head off too far. Make sure you've got the range to come back.

'I do have something here that will help you, though. These small clips,' said Hamish, pointing to a tray that Geordie was now bringing forward. 'If you can wear them, it'd be much appreciated. Get in trouble and there's a button on them you can press, and we'll come to your assistance. If, however, something happens to you and you're not back here at night, then we'll come and look for you. It also sets off an alarm if you disappear into the water. So yes, take them off while swimming, and I suggest you don't swim alone. You have at least somebody who knows where you are and expects you back. But we're all big boys and girls. I'm sure we can handle that.'

Geordie came round with the tray, and Hope took one that had her name tagged below it. John put one on as well, and Hope was interested to note that there was also one for little Ian, but she doubted it would be needed. She called Hamish over.

'Do you mind if he doesn't wear this? It's just that he'll play with it and set it off, and you'll be running around everywhere. He'll be with one of us at all times. We will not leave him.'

'Fine,' said Hamish. 'That's fine, as long as you're happy with that.' Hope handed the tag back, and heard little Ian gurgling.

'You need feeding.'

'If you wish,' said Hamish to the group, 'you can come out with me for a quick walk.'

Hope stood up, but could feel that Ian was getting restless. Thankfully, Hamish only took them outside briefly, pointing up to Boreray, the rocky island the structure was attached to.

'On the far side, there's a shooting range. Please feel free to go up. If you haven't handled a weapon before, I will happily come and spend some time teaching you. There are traps there to fire the clay pigeons. There's also a large seabird colony on the other side of the island. You're more than welcome to walk around the island. We have some viewing points set up as well. There's a golf tee, which you can drive off into the water if you wish. And there's a small observatory, from which at night you can look up at the stars with a rather powerful telescope. If you need to know how it's operated, again, talk to me. We'll make sure somebody is there.'

Hamish brought the guests back inside, and then turned and said, 'That's it. That's the tour. This is your place, your holiday. Please engage me at any time for any of your needs, as well as Ella, Geordie, Ollie, Helena and Christophe. I hope you have a wonderful stay.'

With that, Hamish stepped to one side, and some guests talked among themselves. Hope looked for a chair and sat down. 'He needs fed,' she said to John. 'You think I should go back to the pod?'

'It's our holiday. That's what he said. You want to feed him? We feed him here. You're not indiscreet about it. You don't have to feel awkward.'

'It's funny,' said Hope. 'I feel a little like we're imposters. We're not meant to be here. We're not—'

'What, rich? Stuff that,' said John. 'Go on, feed away. I'll engage the other people. See if I can find a few to talk to.'

Hope sat down, adjusted herself so that Ian could feed and then sat back. Although she was on holiday, the instincts of a lifetime didn't change, and she began studying the guests. There appeared to be only one other couple with a family, and they had two younger kids. As she looked around, a young woman came over to sit beside her.

'How old's your wee one?' said the young woman.

'Oh, barely got started, less than six months, but he's great. He'll be six months in a couple of days.'

'So cool you breastfeed him,' said the woman. 'Some of my sisters didn't.'

'Well, it's up to each mother, isn't it?' said Hope. 'I thought it was right, so I did it.'

'Do I recognise you?' asked the woman.

'I don't know—do you?' asked Hope.

'Sorry,' she said. 'My name's Laura. I'm Laura Blaze. I'm here with Paul. He owns his own company.'

'I'm Hope. Here with John. I'm Hope McGrath. I'm a detective.'

'That's how I know you. I've seen you on the telly.'

'I have to do press conferences and all that. But please keep it quiet. I just want to be a mum.'

'Yes, you're the tall red-haired woman. Wow. And you've got a kid now too. I wonder why I hadn't seen you. That other guy was on recently. What do they call him?'

'DCI Macleod.'

'Macleod. He's so grumpy. You were much better up there.'

Hope nearly burst out laughing. 'He's not really like that,' she said. 'He's a decent man.'

'Yeah, but he's not made for the telly, is he?'

Hope thought that was unfair. There was a time when Seoras—well, they hadn't got close in that way. She was very fond of him.

'What does your husband do?' asked Laura.

'He used to run a car firm,' said Hope. 'We won a competition to be here. We don't own a big business.'

'Well, I don't own one either. Paul's the CEO of his own company. I'm lucky to be here, I guess. He brought me out here for a reason. I'm not sure why. I think he might be going to propose.'

'Wow,' said Hope. 'What a place to do it.'

'I know, isn't it amazing?' said Laura. 'It's just fantastic. But

I can't be sure. I'll not mention your being a detective.'

Hope was feeling tired, and with Ian feeding as well, she didn't listen particularly well. She'd have to sort that out when she was back on the job. But for a while, she just let Laura talk. The woman was lovely, in fairness. Young, very early twenties, Hope thought. She had long black hair and a curvy figure. But in fairness, she didn't seem like a gold digger. She talked about Paul, from what Hope listened to, with a certain affection.

Hope suddenly started. There was a row happening near the bar. She saw two men, both with drinks beside them, suddenly having a go at each other. She couldn't hear exactly what the row was about, but it was certainly intense. There was some pulling of arms by the women who were with them, telling him to calm down. A few other men raised hands, saying it was enough. And then Hamish stepped over.

He's fantastic, Hope thought, *in diffusing the situation. Not having a go at them, but seeming to remind them where they were, seeming to point out the various areas where they could keep space between each other.* It had been a long day, and Hope thought she would need some food soon, but the little guy had gone to sleep again. John arrived back and was introduced to Laura, who then disappeared off to get hold of Paul.

'Take him back to the pod,' said Hope. 'He needs to sleep. Maybe we can get dinner separately.'

'Or we can get our order to our chef to make it. I'm sure we can bring it down to the pod. That won't be a problem. We can do what we want,' said John. 'That's what they said. Or take him into one of those rooms.'

'I just don't want him waking up with that noise we just had. Ian needs his sleep at the moment or he'll be hell.'

They made their way back to the pod, and once inside, Hope

turned to John. 'What was that about? Those two guys kicking off.'

'Too much alcohol. Big business owners. I don't know,' said John. 'Arses, really.'

'That was it, was it? Just boys?'

'Well,' said John, 'from what I could gather, the two of them didn't realise they'd be here together at the same time.'

'I thought they owned the place,' said Hope, 'from what was being said.'

'Maybe they didn't want to be here together. I don't know,' said John. 'Anyway, Hamish seemed to have sorted it out. Although he still looked pretty pissed when they separated.'

'Well, if we eat at the main lounge, we'll take one of the side rooms. And yes, let's get Ollie to make us dinner. I fancy that.'

'For two weeks you can get treated like a queen,' said John.

'Just right,' she said. 'Absolutely. I think this is going to be good.'

Chapter 05

Hope lay in the bed, with arms wrapped around her. She felt John nuzzling up to her, and then he was gone. There was a sheet lying across her hips, but the warmth of the room meant that she was quite happy. And then, a blast of chilly air suddenly rolled across the bed.

She gave a quick shiver, opened her eyes, and looked over towards the pod's window. It was rising, moving back, opening up the pod to the air. Across the room, John was standing.

'This what you wanted? What you need? Skinny dip in the morning!' he shouted. Hope laughed at him, wrapping herself up, feeling the cold air around her. But she watched John jumping out of their pod and into the sea. He came scrambling back in a moment later.

'Unbelievable,' he said. 'That is so cold.'

He pressed a button, and the window began its slow process of closing again. John made for the shower, and Hope heard the water coming on and his scream of delight at warm water. She sat up and looked over at the cot beside her where little Ian was still asleep, though she wondered how. Throwing off the bedclothes, she wandered around and opened the shower room door.

'You're insane,' she said.

'That's what you wanted to do. You're insane. I needed to see just how nuts this woman I'm in love with is.'

Hope laughed, but heard Ian beginning to whimper in his cot. She turned, picked the child up and held him close. Yes, this was going to be a wonderful holiday.

Having both dressed, John and Hope made their way to the main lounge to seek some breakfast. Hope took some fresh fruit and yoghurt and sat down opposite John who had been supplied with an omelette by Ollie. As Hope ate, she held little Ian John on her knee, and they were soon joined by the family with young kids.

'I haven't said hello yet,' said the woman. 'Excuse me, my name's Hannah. This is Ivor, and these are the kids. You're the guys that won the competition, aren't you?'

'That's us,' said Hope. 'I'm Hope McGrath. This is John, my partner, and this is little Ian John.'

'Oh, he's lovely,' said Hannah, and then looked across at her husband. 'I think the alternative milks are down in that fridge in the far corner.' He nodded and walked over. 'Ivor's got a milk intolerance. Carries an EpiPen. He has to be careful, but there's plenty of good stuff out here for him. And with a proper chef on hand too. Still, when you pay for this, that's what you'd expect.'

Hannah got some cereal for her kids before coming back and sitting down beside Hope.

'Well, I hope you enjoy it,' she said, 'because to be honest, it cost a fortune putting this together. I'm lucky with Ivor's job. He's a CEO in a large company.'

'What sort of company?' asked Hope.

'Construction. He's done a lot of work in South America,

but we're just here for a break. It's nice to get away. Pity about those guys shouting the other day, but as long as they don't bother us. Anyway, your little guy's lovely. Have a good day.'

Hannah went off to attend to her kids. Ivor seemed to mosey over different milk that he'd found in the fridge.

'Why doesn't he just get the guy to make him something?' asked John. 'I mean, Ollie's a proper chef. He'll know what to do.'

'Some people like to do things for themselves, don't they?' said Hope. 'And sometimes they like to make things themselves—don't trust anybody else to make it as well.'

'Well, not this guy. This omelette was fantastic. What are we going to do today?' asked John.

'Why don't we take a walk? Yeah? Take a walk around. We've kind of been stuck in the pod so far, but the day looks like it's going to be all right out there. Brisk, yes, but okay.'

'As long as we wrap up the wee man,' said John.

Half an hour later, Hope and John had stepped outside of the main construction and onto the island of Boreray. Ian was in the baby carrier, underneath John's jacket, snuggling up to his father. Hope loved the view of the two of them as she walked hand in hand with John up the steep slopes of Boreray.

Above them was the shooting range, a large construct on the far side, which appeared to be mainly wood. There was a sign saying 'The Lodge' over the top of it, but Hope directed John away from it as they moved over towards the cliffs. It was hard to see down them, to where all the seabirds were, but you could hear the noise they made. The couple walked along and up to a viewpoint, a little constructed shelter, from where they could see the observatory too.

'There's not really much room to go for a run, is there?' said

Hope.

'Why would you want to go for a run? You can just stand and look at this,' said John.

'Guess there's a gym though, isn't there?'

'I can't see people coming this far without a gym. I don't remember Hamish saying it, though. No doubt there will be if there isn't any already.'

As they walked back towards the main buildings, Hope looked down at the tiny floating harbour and the pontoons with the kayaks and the boats.

'Why don't you take a kayak out?' said Hope. 'You like to go kayaking. Give you a bit of time out there. I'll hang on to him.'

'No,' said John. 'You're going back to work. You need a rest before doing so.'

'We both need a rest, John. You're the one who's going to have to be looking after him. You're the one who's—'

'You need a rest. You need away, time to get that head clear. And if you stay here with him, you'll be thinking about who these people are. You've already started to do it, I know.'

'Okay,' said Hope. She walked back to the pod with John before changing into a wetsuit. When she came out, down towards the pontoons, she saw Laura was there as well. Hope still had her little device clipped to her that would say where she was and she noted Laura had hers on too.

'Oh, I was going to go kayaking on my own. Do you want to come out with me?' Laura asked.

'Is Paul busy?' asked Hope.

'He doesn't enjoy kayaking. I think he has some things to think over. I'm not sure. Anyway, I'm just going to get out in the kayak and enjoy this island.'

'Well, I wanted to see the seabirds,' said Hope, 'but I couldn't from the cliff top. I guess we'd maybe get a better view if we kayaked round there, to the other side of the island.'

'Good idea,' said Laura. Together the two women got into their kayaks, attached the spray decks, and were soon paddling round. Hope was loving the fresh air, and her hair was now tied up again, lest it be blown across her face. As they reached the edge of the island, they looked up, and sure enough, the birds on the island were something spectacular.

'Apparently, it's even more spectacular in mating season. I know there's some here at the moment, but when they come to mate, lay their eggs and raise their young, it's meant to be stunning. I hope Paul's going to come back in the summer.'

'It's a bit of a weird time to be coming here in November,' said Hope.

'Well, they just opened it, you see. Paul said. I guess they all wanted to come and test it out.'

'Well, the two guys who were fighting, they didn't seem to think they were coming together.'

'I don't know how that worked,' said Laura. 'But yes, they seemed annoyed. Paul said not to worry about it. They were always fighting with each other, those two.'

Hope turned back, away from the birds, and along with Laura paddled closer round to the construction. She thought about paddling round and maybe seeing the rear of it again, because they hadn't since the day they docked with the cruiser. In saying that, it wouldn't be long before they were visited again, fresh fruit and supplies to come. Hope found Laura could talk just as well in the water as she could back in the lounge.

'I just can't believe I'm here,' said Laura. 'You know Paul and I split up. We only patched it up recently.'

'Well, that's great,' said Hope. 'I'm glad you got it back together.'

'Well, I was completely surprised,' said Laura. 'You see, he seemed so definite about the breakup, and once Paul starts something, he finishes it. That's the way he is. But he said that he had made a mistake. I'm just so glad because I always wanted him. You know, he's intense, yes, but he's amazing. I wish I could be like you, though.'

'What do you mean?' asked Hope.

'A mother. That sort of cements it, doesn't it?'

'I never really thought of it like that,' said Hope. 'I mean, I've just been with John. Ian hasn't cemented it. We've had a lot more challenges before him. I guess in the old days you'd have cemented it when you got married, but we don't need to be married. John and I have never seen the need for it.'

'I'd love to get married,' said Laura. 'Paul wasn't having it. I mean, I would love to. And then, well, I think he's changed his mind on that. That's why I think he's going to propose. I still think he's going to do it.'

Hope brought her kayak to a halt in the water, and Laura came alongside her.

'What's up?' she asked.

'Over there,' said Hope. 'Those two on the jet skis, is that those two idiots that were arguing the other day?'

'Looks like them. Why?'

'Watch,' said Hope. The two men were turning the jet skis away from each other before turning back on a direct course. They kept coming closer and closer until one would pull out of the way suddenly at the last minute. They were arguing and shouting at each other.

'What is it with them?' asked Hope. 'They're just, what,

egotistical idiots. That's really dangerous. They'll end up killing each other.'

'I think they were going to kill each other last night before Hamish stepped in.'

'And they don't know what they're doing with those jet skis. They don't know how to handle them,' said Hope. She'd been on one before during her holidays, and though she would never call herself an expert, she could certainly handle them a lot better than these guys were.

'They're going at it again,' said Laura. 'Look at that.'

The jet skis turned, but this time there seemed something else about them. As they got closer, Hope thought neither of them were flinching. It was only at the last second that one pulled away, but the other jet ski caught the back end of the one that had turned. Both of the men were thrown off the jet skis into the water. Neither was wearing a life jacket.

'Come on,' said Hope, and tore a paddle into the water, routing as quickly as she could across the water. The jet ski engines had stopped; the tags that instantly killed the engines once somebody had fallen off must have deactivated them. But Hope could only see one man. He was waving his arms frantically.

'Laura, get him,' said Hope, and she paddled over towards the other jet ski. Hope looked around until she thought she could see something under the water.

Oh hell, she thought, and turned her own kayak upside down, pulled away the skirt, and hauled herself out of it. Then she turned around in the water, located herself in the water according to the image she'd thought she'd seen, and swam hard towards it. The man came into her blurred view. Hope grabbed her hand around his waist, driving upwards with her legs. She was a powerful swimmer, but the man wasn't easy to deal with. Hope broke the surface of the sea and then looked around her. Her kayak was a short distance away.

The man she was holding on to, spat water and struggled, which was the last thing Hope needed him to do. She yelled at him to stay still, and tried to swim across to her kayak, but he was making it more and more difficult. As she reached it, she put her hand on it and tried to pull it closer to her. Then, using her legs and kicking hard, she turned the man in her arms towards it, telling him to throw his arms onto the kayak. She pushed him up until he was lying on top of it, draped over it, his head barely out of the water. She looked over and saw Laura with the other man holding onto the side of Laura's kayak.

'That arsehole,' the man on Laura's kayak shouted, 'could have got us killed. You're such an arse.'

The man beside Hope swore an expletive and told the man what he could do with himself.

'Take me over there,' the man said to Laura.

'No, you don't,' said Hope. 'If you two can't behave, you're not getting close together.'

'Do you know who I am?' shouted the man at Hope. 'I don't take orders from a holidaymaker like you.'

I'm DI Hope McGrath. I'm with the police. And if you insult me like that again, sir, I'll arrest you wherever you are. The words rang through Hope's head, but she simply said she'd drop him back in the water. The man glared at her. Hope, meanwhile, was working out how to get them both back to the main structure without killing each other.

It was then that she saw a rowing boat coming towards her. John had the oars. He came up close, and Hope got pulled on board by John. She then pulled her own man on board before reaching for the kayak and attaching it to the boat. She looked and saw her little kid still in the sling around John.

'Couldn't you get anybody else?' she asked, concerned.

'No, his mum was in the water, and we were going,' said John. Hope grinned. Of course, John was right.

'Head over there,' she said. 'I warn you, these two are at each other's throats. I may need to go back to work here.'

'I don't envy them,' said John as he paddled across. Coming alongside Laura's kayak, Hope helped pull the other man into the rowing boat.

'You sit there, and shut up,' said Hope. She was standing up now, all six feet of her, leaning over the man. She turned to the man she'd pulled on board already. 'And you sit over there. I don't want a word out of the pair of you, because if you do, I will throw you back in.'

'Have you got everyone?' asked Laura.

'Let's get back. Laura, go ahead. Tell them we're coming in with having been two in the water. Ask Hamish. We need first-aid attendance.'

'I'm bloody okay,' said one man.

'You bloody well are not,' said Hope. 'And that's my call. The moment you ditched yourself in there needing a rescue, you lost all rights. It's my call. Now sit there and shut up.'

John rowed in, and by the time they'd reached the pontoons, Hamish had arrived. Hope told him the men would need a quick going-over. Both men disappeared separately back towards their pods. By the time Hope had got out, rearranged the kayak, emptied the water out of it, and secured it back to the pontoon, Laura was still there.

'Wow,' she said. 'You really know what you're doing, don't

you?'

'I'm good in the water,' said Hope. 'And I don't take any nonsense. It's the day job.'

'Well that's our secret,' said Laura.

Hamish emerged from the buildings down onto the pontoon. 'They're both okay,' he said, 'and I'm sorry that you had to deal with that. What were they doing?'

'Playing chicken. Chicken with your jet skis, which coincidentally are still out there on the water. You might need somebody to pop out and get them. I can help you with that if you need it.'

'No, no, no, I'll get Helene and Christophe to get them. You've done enough. I apologise for your having had to do that. This is your break,' said Hamish.

'Personally, I wouldn't give them any alcohol.'

'Indeed, but as they paid for the place,' said Hamish, 'they are my masters. It's not so easy to jump in front of them like that.'

'Well, I'm your girl,' said Hope. 'You need any help, you call.'

'Well, we'll see you at dinner tonight,' said Hamish.

'Aren't we making our own, or is it—?'

'Well, you're welcome to do what you want, but our chef, Ollie, has said he will make tonight for everyone, or at least everyone at once. Sit down and have a bit of a get-together.'

'As long as you don't put those two on the same table,' said Hope. Hamish gave a laugh, and John took Hope's hand.

'Come on then, action woman, let's get you warmed up,' said John. 'And by the way,' he whispered, 'that's the last bit of police work you're doing on this holiday.'

Hope gave him a smile. 'Sorry,' she said. 'I just—'

'You save lives. It's what you do,' said John. 'It's okay. But that's the end.'

Hope gave him a kiss. 'Of course,' she said. 'It's not like I'm looking for the work.'

Chapter 06

'Are you going to dress up?' asked John.

'Do you want me to?'

'It's up to you,' said John.

'Do you think the others are going to?'

'Look,' said John. 'I'm not bothered, but if you want to dress up, I'll be quite happy. You've been flopping around in this, that and whatever for these last lot of months, just looking after the wee man. Why don't you dress up?'

'You want me to, don't you?'

'Yes,' said John.

'You know you can say sometimes what you want from me. I don't see it as a problem, you know? I'll do the same to you.'

'You will, will you?'

'I want that shirt on, the one I bought you. The one you don't wear much.'

'Okay,' said John. 'I'll wear it. But you better look good tonight.'

'You told me I look good all the time, especially now I'm a mum.'

'It should be easy then,' said John.

Hope laughed at him but went into her case to find out what

she would wear. She pulled out a rather elegant strapless dress. Hope had thought about wearing it one special night to dinner, but now felt the right time. She needed to feel good about herself, needed to feel, well, what was it, sexy?

John was superb at making her feel happy, comfortable about herself. He always praised her, especially after the changes with the pregnancy. But all the excess weight and then the sheer effort of raising Ian through those first few months left her bedraggled. She wanted to feel like the goddess John told her she was.

It didn't take long before she was ready, and he stood and watched her. She brushed her hair as she stood on heels. That was the only bit she didn't like. Hope was much more comfortable in hiking boots or trainers. After all, that's what she enjoyed doing —running around. Always more of a sports girl than a model, she never wanted to be a princess. Hope wanted to be an athlete. She wanted to be at the top.

John gave a whistle, and she turned around to show him what she was wearing.

'I like the shirt,' she said. 'Where's the wee man?'

Ian was dressed up in a dainty little outfit, and Hope carried him. For a moment she thought John was sad. She looked at John. 'Does this not suit?'

'How can he ever not suit being on you?'

'Why the face then?'

'Because a little bit of us has died. No, grown up. There's no more, us. There's now, *us*. Fantastic as it is, and it is, that early excitement is gone, replaced by something stronger but more at ease. Can't look back. Be great to have it all at once, but I guess the passing is what makes it so precious. Come on,' said John, and he opened the door for her.

They made their way in a rather strange fashion along the pontoon and into the main building. It was strange walking in heels when the pontoon was actually moving, but once she got inside the lounge area, Hope could stand better on them. She was glad she had dressed, for everyone else seemed to be made up to the nines.

The lights were low in the lounge at the moment. Tables had been set out, and Hope and John were led to one with people all around their age. There were three couples in front of them, and as they sat down, they were introduced. Stephen and Tammy Winner were an American couple who owned an umbrella tech company. There were Frederico and Maisie Humphries, a Spanish couple. He was the CEO of a large energy company. Terence and Alicia Juniper were English and came from a rival large energy company. John felt a little embarrassed announcing that he used to run a car-hire firm.

'What about you then?' Hope was asked. She knew Laura had seen her on TV and knew she was a detective but hoped that Laura wouldn't say so. Hope announced she was merely focusing on being a mum. Tammy Winner looked across at little Ian sitting on Hope's lap.

'He's adorable,' she said. 'Isn't he, Stephen? Absolutely adorable.'

'You've started her now. She's going to say we should have brought the kids,' her husband replied.

'Well, we should have. We should have made a family thing of it.'

'Not until I'm sure what it is and how happy I am with it. Might have paid for it, but—'

'Oh, you shouldn't have brought them. We don't bring ours,' said Maisie Humphreys. Although Frederico was Spanish,

Maisie had a very distinctive English accent. 'Oh, Frederico swept me off my feet. Didn't you, at the polo.'

'At the polo?' queried Hope.

'He enjoys polo. We have our own stables,' said Maisie. 'He's very into quality horses, aren't you, Frederico? But we are here to have fun and not to be caught up in the family drag. That's why we have a nanny.'

Frederico didn't seem to speak much, but Maisie certainly made up for him.

'What do your companies do then?' asked Hope turning to the other guests. She saw John looking at her. She was digging. That's what she was doing. She wasn't making polite conversation; she was digging. It's what she did. It was so natural now, she didn't even realise when she was doing it.

'Well, I'm self-made,' said Terence. 'I own a large energy company. I do a lot of the work down in South America. At the end of the day, that's where a lot of it's happening, isn't it? We've won an environmental award for the work that we do in Brazil. But it's not just about preserving nature. You've got to work with nature. After all, we still need our energy.'

'That's correct,' said Stephen. 'We need the tech to do it. High-tech solutions. Effective high-tech solutions. And therefore, we can use the energy, but keep nature too.'

'You've all won awards, have you?' asked Hope.

'Frederico's company has too,' said Maisie. 'He's quite the genius with it.'

'I'll take issue with that,' said Terence. 'I think I can outdo him on that front.'

'They're always like this,' said Maisie. 'Can't be happy just to be all at the top.'

'Well, at least they're not fighting, like those two were earlier on,' said Hope.

'Oh, I heard about that,' said Maisie. 'Apparently, you pulled a few of them out of the water.'

'Yes, wasn't good. Was it that Ivor?' said Maisie. 'Ivor and Corey, from what I heard.'

'It could be any of them,' said Alicia suddenly. Alicia was quite a small woman, softly spoken, with blonde hair. Unlike Maisie, she was incredibly confident, and whilst a large woman, she carried tons of charisma. Tammy, however, was capable of taking over the conversation, and the American looked at Hope.

'You could have done well for yourself, girl. Go and grab these guys, on their way up, knowing what they're doing. It's difficult being a wife to them. But you know what? It's worth it. You see the passion and the fire in them.'

'Oh, there's plenty of fire in John,' said Hope.

'Well, what's he going to do then?'

'John's just finding his way at the moment before he launches into his next thing,' said Hope. 'I'm just going to keep an eye on our kid here.'

'Wouldn't you want to be coming here all the time, though?' said Tammy. 'Wouldn't you want to be owning this? It's so good to be away.'

'One thing I don't understand,' said Hope. 'Why didn't you put it somewhere like the Maldives? Why not?'

'Everybody's got a place in the Maldives. But look at this. It's stunning. It really is a retreat away from a retreat. You don't get anybody out here. Who's going to come? And then, when you get those fine days, you put that pod lid back, and you can lie here. A place where your heart's content. You've got everything around you that you need.'

'Wouldn't you ever get bored out here?' asked Hope. 'I mean, don't take me the wrong way. But if you're out here all the time—'

'It's a retreat,' said Terrence. 'It's a way to get away from all the hassle. It's difficult when you run your own company. I guess you wouldn't understand what it is to have hassle in your life.'

The man's never been a police detective, thought Hope. *He doesn't understand what hassle is, and he doesn't understand what it's like to have people's lives in your hands.*

'I think there's more to life than running big companies,' said John. 'I do like the conservation angle though. Have any of you ever gone down yourselves, been part of it, close to the bone?'

'Been on visits,' said Tammy. 'Far too busy to get on with actually spending time down there.'

Yet you're here for a couple of weeks, thought Hope. *Not that busy.*

When the food arrived, Hope was truly blown away. The meal was splendid. She'd never tasted food like it. How what looked like simple fare danced across her tongue, whipping the taste buds into a frenzy. She could tell John enjoyed that side of it, but not so much the conversation. *It won't matter*, thought Hope. For the rest of the trip, they could stay on their own.

The evening moved on, and soon everyone had finished their meal. A little light music was put on, and some danced in the middle of the lounge, but Hope could tell John was feeling awkward. She made excuses, saying that they needed to get Ian off to bed and take care of him. But when they reached the pod, John was thanking her.

'What a bunch of arseholes,' he said, entering.

'It's not our world, is it?' said Hope.

'It's the way they talk down to me. You know? Oh, we're the holidaymakers. We're the plebs who won this. I don't understand why they even bothered to have us come along.'

'They're not all like that. Laura's quite nice.'

'You said she's the girlfriend, though. She hasn't been married in. Not been institutionalised. She doesn't know how to be rude to people yet.'

Hope hit him. 'Stop that,' she said. 'Anyway, you can get out of that shirt now. I know it was killing you all night to wear it.'

'It's not me,' said John, and then he touched Hope from behind. 'But you are,' he said. He took the straps of her dress and pushed them off her shoulders. And then they heard a whimper from Ian.

'You're kidding me, aren't you?' said John. 'You're kidding me; we've sat there, had that meal and everything, and not once has he looked for food. As soon as I get back here—'

'Yep,' said Hope. 'He knows how to sort his dad out, doesn't he?' She let the dress slip off and then sat on the bed, bringing her wee one over to feed him. John lay down on the bed beside them.

'You could have told him you were a police officer. You could have told him about all the cases you solved,' he said. 'But you said you were just continuing to be a mum. Why didn't you?'

'They're not worth it. Laura knows. I told her. But only her, as she's normal. I don't want to share my joys, my successes with people. They don't give two hoots for them,' said Hope. 'I want to share them with people who mean something. Laura's a nice girl. But I wonder about him. I haven't seen him with her that much. Not like you. Can't get you off me.'

'Is that a bad thing?' asked John.

'No,' said Hope. 'Of course not.' They lay there, until eventually Ian had to be winded. After several loud burps, they placed him down in his cot. 'Early night then,' said Hope. She rolled off the bed, stripped down and then got back into it, and John copied her.

'Are you tired?' he said.

'Yes,' said Hope. John moved over, held her tight, and Hope listened to him breathing. He clearly wasn't going to sleep.

'Are you ready for it?'

'For what?' asked Hope, thinking he was playing a game.

'Macleod going. Are you ready for who comes next? You've kind of, well, the two of you form a heck of a team. So used to each other now.'

'We're just partners. We just work together.'

'Might be partners, but those three sitting at the table tonight, they all worked in South America. Maybe they've won conservation awards together but they didn't look like partners, though. You and Macleod are so comfortable working with each other.'

'You've not seen me shout at him, or have a go at him.'

'And I bet you he takes it and listens.'

'Usually. Sometimes he shouts back.'

'Because you know each other. Are you going to be ready for what comes next?'

'Well, he is older than I am. He's got to go sometime,' said Hope. 'And he's trusted me with his team. He's not doing the same job he was when we met, nor am I. I'm the boss. You remember that. I'm the boss. You have to manage your DCI. You have to manage the ones above. That's what Seoras always said. He always told me I had to handle them. Handle them my way. He'd have called them out tonight. He'd have just told them straight. Not me.'

'Do you know something?' said John. 'Every night since that wee one's been born, I have been so shattered. I don't feel shattered tonight.'

'Me neither,' said Hope. 'Me neither.' And she turned to face him.

Chapter 07

'Is he still asleep?' asked John.

'Yes,' said Hope. 'Out like a light. Look at him, though. That's what you want.'

'Not a problem though,' said John. 'Not with the view I've got here.'

Hope looked towards the window and then saw that John was staring at her. 'That's so cheesy,' she said. 'Don't be cheesy.' She rolled over in the bed and gave him a cuddle. Then her stomach rumbled.

'Somebody's got the munchies,' said John playfully.

'I'll be fine,' she said, and rolled away from him, only for her stomach to rumble again.

'Get something to eat,' said John. 'I'll stay here with Ian. Besides, I'm not hungry. I don't need to eat as much as you.'

For that, he got a pillow in the face, and Hope rolled out of bed and made her way to the shower. A few minutes later, she came back, dressed in a light pair of tracksuit bottoms and a t-shirt, before standing over her boy again.

'I could watch him like that all day,' she said. 'Just sleeping. He's just so cute.' Again, her stomach rumbled.

'Eat something before you wake him up,' said John.

Hope slipped feet into trainers, and then made her way out of the pod, across the pontoon, and into the lounge area. She thought she was properly hungry, and would have a bowl of muesli, or possibly even some porridge. But then she saw the croissants.

She strode over, put a couple on a plate, and then saw that some bacon had been done beside them. She took some of that as well, and then some mushrooms, and then sat down and thought, if she didn't stop eating, she would eat so much she'd balloon. Hope wasn't normally a big eater, but when the food was there, and it looked so good, it was hard to refuse. And who cared anyway? After these two weeks, she'd be back to the police station canteen. While it wasn't awful, and was more than adequate, it wasn't at this level of catering.

Hope sat down and saw various guests arrive. She gave a nod to them, but she failed to spot Ivor and Hannah. They were usually up early these last couple of days; the kids got them up. But there were no signs. She continued to eat, but still they didn't appear. And after a bit, Hamish passed by. Hope reached out to him.

'Hamish, you haven't seen Ivor and Hannah, have you? Those kids are usually up and running around.'

'Oh my gosh, you won't have heard, will you? We had an unfortunate incident last night.'

The hair on the back of Hope's neck pricked up. 'An incident?'

'Yes,' said Hamish. 'Ivor seems to have taken a reaction last night. A very serious one.'

'Well, he's milk intolerant.'

'However he managed it, it seems he ingested something that wasn't good for him. We took him to the medical quarters, but in the night, it was decided that he needed to get to the mainland for some attention. So, we flew him out along with Hannah and the kids.'

Hope looked around and noted that one or two of the kids' toys were still there. It was annoying to her that the staff hadn't tidied up, but now she wondered why they had collected nothing to go with them. Hamish spied where she was looking.

'There wasn't time to get everything together. I'll be gathering everything up and moving it on,' said Hamish. 'I wouldn't worry about it. I'm sure he'll be perfectly fine. It's one of those things though they needed to get him hospital attention just to make sure. I can do a lot out here, and I have a bit of medical knowledge, but I'm nothing compared to a trained doctor in a hospital.'

'Of course,' said Hope. 'That's a terrible shame though. I think the kids were enjoying it out here. I think they were too, Ivor and Hannah.'

'Well, what's not to enjoy?' said Hamish. 'But that's life, isn't it. Wherever you go, something can always happen, and that's why we're prepared. We don't like to put it in the guests' faces, which is why all the emergency radio equipment and other gear is kept back at the staff quarters. So don't worry. Everything all right with you?'

'It's been fine,' said Hope. 'I've been enjoying it, to be honest. Have our friends calmed down any?'

'I think you're asking a bit more from me than can be done,' said Hamish. 'I try to keep them quiet. It's like I say though, when they pay for something, when they own it, it's not that easy for someone like me to quieten them down.'

'I don't envy you,' said Hope, laughing. 'By the way, you can tell Ollie that these croissants are just divine, especially with the bacon.'

'He puts maple syrup in with the bacon. Such a fantastic cook.'

'He really is,' said Hope. 'Wish I could afford this all the time.'

'To be honest,' said Hamish, 'if you could, you probably wouldn't appreciate it, like our two rowing factions. I didn't say that, by the way. They pay my bills, so zip on that.'

Hamish disappeared, and Hope sat back with a coffee. John hadn't come through with the little one, which must have meant he was still asleep. On that basis, Hope would let him sleep. John had told her to sit and eat, and that's what she was doing. John was good like that. He was always ready to give her space, always ready to allow her a bit of time. She never felt she was left with her child, though she wanted to be with him so much. He'd wake up soon though, and that required Mum. Food time. She would just enjoy her time before the demands of Ian took precedence.

'Hi,' said a voice.

Hope looked around and saw Laura approaching her. The young woman looked exhausted.

'Are you okay?' asked Hope.

'I'm more than okay,' she said with a smile on her face. 'Let me get something. Okay?'

'Of course,' said Hope. She watched as the girl, who was dressed in a short skirt and t-shirt, glided along the prepared food. She was accumulating a large plate of just about everything, and placed it down on the table that Hope sat at. Laura got some fruit juice, as well as coffee. When she sat back down, she instantly tucked into her croissants.

'Hungry?'

'Didn't get much sleep last night,' said Laura, and then gave a smile.

Hope didn't like to think of herself as being old, but she was past the very initial stage, where John and she didn't leave each other alone. They certainly weren't dead, dead as far as the physicality of the relationship was. More just exhausted, thanks primarily to the results of the previously more excitable time.

'It's done wonders for us out here,' said Laura. 'Paul's, well, he's got that look in his eye again. I'd lost that with him. I'd lost that urge where he wanted me, you know? You know that feeling?'

Hope smiled. She wondered why the woman was telling her all this, but then again, who else was she going to talk to? Hope was somebody who would disappear and never be seen in the same company again after these couple of weeks. If Laura were married to Paul, no doubt she'd be seeing some of the rest of them. Maybe she didn't want to talk about such things with them.

'It was all quite excitable last night,' she said.

'Yes, I hear Ivor had to be taken away,' said Hope, quickly changing the subject before she got too much detail about Laura's night.

'Yes,' said Laura suddenly. 'What a commotion! He just, well, he just dropped. Hamish and the staff were brilliant. Absolutely amazing. He went down on the floor as if he were having a fit. And then Hannah hit him with the EpiPen. She'd clearly done it before. But then, when he was sort of half recovered, they moved him out into the medical area. Didn't let the rest of us come through. But Hamish came back and gave us updates. He said that when they took them through, he was in touch with the doctor over there. And then the doctor said they needed to take him back to the mainland for observation to be sure. It was all very exciting. And then Paul, well, Paul wined and dined me last night. Danced me here, there, and everywhere. And then we were back, back at our pod.'

'So, when did they take away Ivor?'

'I don't know,' said Laura. 'I mean, I don't think I slept last night. I can't remember having slept. Can remember a lot of other things.' She laughed. 'But it couldn't have been a helicopter they took him in. They must have taken him on a boat. Because you hear those things, don't you? Helicopters, when they arrive.'

You certainly do, thought Hope. *And actually, there wasn't a helicopter pad here. Where would they land?* The island to which the structure was attached was very steep. She wasn't sure if you could set a helicopter down on it. The structure itself had no helipad that Hope knew of, only serviced by boat. Maybe that was deliberate, although Hope thought it also rather strange.

'They certainly make a racket,' said Hope. In her time as a police officer, she'd seen the rescue helicopter, either being on search duty or landing to assist and take away a patient. They were much noisier than the small air ambulances. And you wouldn't have got an air ambulance out here. This was quite a trek. It surely would be the Coastguard who would come.

'Are you sure there wasn't a helicopter?' asked Hope.

'Like I said, I didn't hear one. Maybe they've brought a boat if he wasn't that bad. Maybe they couldn't get the helicopter. Who knows?' said Laura. 'Can't land a helicopter here, can you?'

'No,' said Hope. 'But you can drop a paramedic down and

they can soon pick somebody up. They do it from boats. They don't need to land.'

'That would have been exciting. I guess everybody would have run out to look at it.'

Laura was now tucking back into her food again, ravenous as anything. Hope found it funny, the girl looking to build up her stamina. Part of her felt jealous of Laura. Those times with John were gone. There was the little one in her life. By the time the little one was grown up and out of the house, well, maybe the two of them would want a cup of coffee together rather than a night under the sheets. Hope laughed at herself. And then saw Hamish come in.

'Hello, everyone. I just wanted to announce to you that Ivor's doing fine. He's recovering at the hospital. They're going to keep him for a couple of days, and he won't be coming back, because of the condition he's in. However, he's out of the woods. He's perfectly fine. And I wished him all the best from all of us here. So if any of you are worried, no need to worry at all.' Hamish gave a smile and left the room.

'Well, that's good news, isn't it, Laura?' said Hope.

'Have you ever seen somebody just collapse?' said Laura. 'It was weird. It's like there's no effort to protect yourself as you fall. You just go straight down. Hannah went into action, full flow. She just takes that EpiPen and drives it in. It was quite something. It really was quite something.'

'I've seen it happen before,' said Hope, and she thought she'd seen much worse in her life. People getting stabbed with things other than EpiPens. And she smiled at the young girl beside her.

'Are you doing anything today?' asked Laura. 'Have you got plans?'

'My little one's currently asleep, and when he wakes up, he's going to demand that Mum feed him. I'm going to let John go for a walk out today, do something. He let me get away yesterday to do the kayaking.'

'But that wasn't exactly a break by the end, was it?' said Laura. 'You were quite something.'

'Thanks,' said Hope. 'I've been a strong swimmer all my life. It's something I've just done.'

'Quite a little Mum hero, though. Well, bet the little guy would have loved seeing you.'

Hope hadn't thought about things like that. How would little Ian think of her? His mum, the detective. What would he think of his dad? The house husband. *That's a terrible term*, thought Hope. *He's just a husband. He's just a dad, like other women are not housewives—they're mums.*

She excused herself from Hannah and decided she needed to return to the pod. There was something about little Ian when he needed to feed, something within Hope that clicked, said 'yes, yes, he does.' When she entered the pod, Ian was sitting on his dad's lap, crying.

'Well, that's uncanny,' said John.

'I've told you before, I know.' Hope sat down on the bed, took Ian and began to feed him. She looked over at John. 'Ivor and Hannah have been taken away.'

'Taken away? What, like for fighting?' teased John.

'No, no, no. Ivor had a reaction. He's milk intolerant. Apparently, it was bad. She had to hit him with an EpiPen. He was taken away to the mainland overnight, but I was talking to Lauren. She didn't hear a helicopter coming. I didn't hear a helicopter. You would hear one of those beasts. I mean, they are big, especially the ones they'd send out here.'

'Well, maybe they sent a boat. Maybe not that big of an emergency.'

'You wouldn't, you wouldn't do that. You would just send a helicopter and take him back. If they needed him for observation, if they required to watch him, you don't send a boat out. And besides, they have got no boats.'

'The NHS haven't got any boats, but I bet you there are plenty of boats that would come out and pick them up. These guys have got money, Hope. You've got to remember that,' said John.

'No,' she said. 'I don't like it. Something smells funny about it.'

'We're on a break. You're on a break. In two weeks' time, you can knock yourself out,' said John. 'Two weeks' time, go crazy. Right now, rest up. Switch off. You never switch off,' he said, suddenly quite serious.

'I don't switch on either,' said Hope. 'It's just what is. It's the way I am. It's why I'm so good at it.'

'And so bad at relaxation. Switch off. Focus on this wee man.'

'And his dad, too,' said Hope. She leaned over and gave John a kiss. 'Why don't you head off today? Go up to the shooting range. Why don't you try it?'

'Never really done shooting. Not since I was a young lad.'

'Well, come on, we're not paying for this. Do it. I'll keep Junior here. Plenty I can do kicking about, keeping the wee man entertained.'

'Okay,' said John. 'But remember, you're on a break.'

Chapter 08

John strode out into what was a bracing environment. This far away from the mainland, when the wind blew, it had very little to break it up. As John cleared the main structure, he stepped onto the firm land of Boreray. There was a path marked across the grass that Hope and he had walked previously, which went up to the shooting range on the other side. It was a steep climb up, and John felt a little bit of a chill, for he only had a small jacket on.

It looked like rain would be on the way soon. Despite this, he persevered. There was a lot running through his mind at the moment. After all, he soon would have little Ian full time. Hope would be off and away. Previously, it had never been a problem. If she were away, John could handle that. He knew what she was doing, knew why she was doing it. He didn't have anyone else to explain to. And he just found things to do.

Now, he'd have a little one who would wonder where Mum was. She'd wanted to keep the feeding up as well. But that was going to be a problem when you couldn't tell where she was going to be or when she would get called out here, there, wherever. How would they keep the child fed? So, they had talked about this, about when the child would move over. What was best for Ian? John would have to learn how to prepare a bottle.

In truth, part of him was looking forward to it. He'd had the daily grind of dealing with irate punters who'd hired cars, scraped them and then didn't like the idea of having to pay the excess. He was as proud as punch of Hope, and also a little bemused that she was with him. John didn't think of himself as anything special, but he thought she was very special. And now that she was a mum, he was in awe of her.

In truth, he'd gone off to the shooting range simply to keep Hope happy. Having met most of the people here, they weren't John's type. Businessmen, and the arguing just did his head in, but he would go up and he would show face.

The shooting range was quite impressive though, and as he arrived at the door to the main range, he could hear a boisterous crowd beyond it. On opening the door, John could see Stephen Winner, Federico Humphries, and Terence Juniper, with whom they'd shared a table previously. Also there were Paul Walton and Corey Denman.

'Uh-huh, it's our tourist,' said Stephen Winner. 'You want to handle one of these?' The man was standing with a shotgun, and John was sure it shouldn't be pointing at anyone.

'No,' said John. 'Never used it before.'

'Well, it's time to learn,' said Terence. 'Always does a man good to learn to shoot.'

'Why?' asked John.

'Builds character. Lets you learn how to handle power. How to take charge.'

John was a little bemused by this. He also noticed behind him many liquor bottles. Whisky seemed to be the primary order of the day at the moment, but there were beers as well. He felt awkward about this. After all, they were handling weapons.

'Ah, is it too early in the morning for you?' said Terence. Corey Denman put his hand on Terence's shoulder and walked past to say hello to John.

'I'm a bit of a visitor, like yourself, John,' said Corey. 'I don't own a company like most of these people. I work with them, though, down in South America. That's why I've got the invite up here.'

'And he's got Sylvia with him,' said Terence.

'Terence, she's a bit of something, isn't she?'

'If I were going to pay for somebody to be here, I would have her,' said Stephen suddenly.

John was not comfortable with the direction the chatter was going.

'You don't need to pay for anybody, do you? Child with her as well. She's quite something. Big redhead,' said Corey. 'You've done well for yourself there. Punched above your weight, if you don't mind me saying.'

John minded him saying it, but he did not want to rock the boat, so he just gave a smile.

'You're back with that Laura again, aren't you?' Terence said to Paul.

'She knows what she likes.'

There was a bawdy shout, and a yell, and then Terence turned back to John. 'Do you want to shoot? We're having a little bit of a gamble.'

'You're shooting for money?' said John. 'Never shot before.'

'Well, we're not putting much on the line, five hundred at a time.'

John looked at them. 'Five hundred?' he said. 'Pounds?'

'Yes,' said Corey. 'Five hundred pounds at a time we're

getting down. You up for it?'

'Without being funny, gentlemen,' said John, 'I haven't got five hundred pounds to risk; my salary isn't yours. If you remember, I won this break.'

'Of course, of course,' said Terence. 'No need to be like that. Why don't we then bet on John? One bets whether he's going to hit the clays.'

'Well, let's see him shoot then,' said Corey. John was pushed forward.

'First, though, get some alcohol into him. You always shoot better when you're more relaxed.' This was Stephen talking, and he half stumbled over towards John. 'What will it be? Triple whiskey? Bourbon?'

'I'm not really a beer man at this time of the morning.'

'Don't have to be beer,' said Terence. 'Get a whiskey. Get the man a whiskey.'

A large tumbler of whiskey was put in front of John. He reckoned there must be at least four shots in there, if not five. He took it to his lips and took a small sip. John was sure it must have been the good stuff, but he wasn't particularly big on alcohol.

'Corey, show him what to do with the weapon,' said Terence.

Corey took John to one side, demonstrated the shotgun in front of him, showed him how to load it, and then put it up to his shoulder and fired. John's ears were nearly deafened.

'Don't forget to put the earmuffs on him. You'll blow the poor guy's ears off,' shouted Terence. Everyone laughed loudly.

'We have clay pigeons,' said Corey. 'You shout "Pull", we press a button, and the clay pigeon comes out. Watch!' Corey turned with his gun, looking out through the range towards the sea that was raging below the cliff.

'Pull!' shouted Corey.

Two clay discs whipped out towards the sea. Corey fired twice in quick succession. One exploded, and the other sailed on.

'That's a man who can't hold his drink,' said Terence. 'How did you miss that?'

Corey was undeterred and turned back to John. 'So, you can see what to do, can't you?'

'Okay,' said John, and hunted for some air defenders. He found a pair and put them on. Turning back to Corey, he found the shotgun already loaded for him.

'I thought it'd be easier if I just got you ready. Be aware that it will kick hard. Okay?'

'He'll never hit it in a month of Sundays,' said Terence.

'Well,' said a Spanish voice, 'I think he will. Have faith. He's a Scotsman, after all.' In the background, Federico, the CEO of the rival energy company to Terence, sipped on his whisky. 'Two thousand says he'll hit one of them with his first go.'

'Having a laugh,' said Terence. 'Three thousand says he doesn't.'

Federico walked over to John and looked him up and down. He gave him a smile and a pat on the shoulder. 'A man like this, who can bag a redhead like his wife, can do just about anything,' laughed Frederico.

'She's not my wife,' said John. 'She's my partner.'

'She's yours. You have a kid,' said Frederico. He slapped John on the side. 'You're a man who understands how to get the finer things in life. He will hit. Five thousand says he will hit on the first go.'

'You taking on multiple bets?' asked Stephen. 'I'll match that five.'

'I'll go six,' said Terence.

'Easy, guys,' said John.

Corey tapped him on the shoulder. 'Eh, I wouldn't get involved. This'll escalate. They're just going to do it anyway.'

Slowly the money built up, and John realised they'd put twenty thousand pounds on whether John was going to hit a clay having never truly shot before in his life.

'Remember,' said Frederico. 'I trust you.'

'I don't,' said Terence. 'It'll be my money.'

'I don't trust him either,' said Stephen.

'What about you, Paul?' asked Terence. Paul Walton walked over to John, and stared at him.

'Yes, I'll take the bet,' he said. 'Twenty thousand he misses.'

Corey was laughing now. 'I'll not take the bet,' he said. 'I'll be independent here, make sure John has every chance.'

'Excellent,' said Frederico. He picked up a glass, which must have had at least a triple whiskey in it, and downed it. 'Remember, aim true, my friend!' John was suddenly standing alone, except for Corey. The men stepped back, and Corey brought John forward with the loaded shotgun.

'When you're ready, shout "Pull!"' said Corey. 'I'll press the button. And you just follow the targets. You aim by looking down, and you see the little nock at the end of the shotgun? That's what you keep trained on the clay. Keep the gun pressed into your shoulder.'

John thought this was insane, but then he was in a different world. Best just to get it done with because if he pulled out now, he had the feeling it would just erupt and become much bigger than what it already was. And these guys could probably stand to lose twenty thousand.

John planted his feet and put the butt of the shotgun against his shoulder. He looked down the barrel to the nock at the end. 'It'll come out from over there?' he asked, pointing off to his left.

'From that side,' said Corey. 'The height, the angle's unknown. That's the point.'

'I'll make sure it's one of the wired ones,' said Terence.

'No,' said Frederico. 'He goes on the basics. The man's never shot before.'

'That wasn't stipulated in the bet. That wasn't . . .'

'I'll determine the rules,' said Corey. 'It will be the basic one. When you're ready, John.'

John swallowed hard. He'd do his best, but he wasn't hopeful. 'Pull!'

Two grey discs whizzed into the air. John ignored the one that came out quickest, instead focusing on the other. He moved with it as best he could and then pulled the trigger. He thought his shoulder was going to rip off him and he stumbled backwards.

'He clipped it!' yelled Frederico.

'Bullshit,' said Terence. 'Utter poppycock.'

'No,' said Frederico. 'He hit it, didn't he, Corey?'

'I think a piece may have gone,' said Corey. 'Did you hit it, John?'

'I've no idea,' said John. 'When I fired, it drove my shoulder back. I couldn't see anything. Totally no idea. Sorry.'

'He missed it,' said Terence. 'I agree,' said Stephen.

'You would agree. You bet he would miss,' said Federico. 'Corey, your decision. You are the one judging this.'

'I think he clipped it. Barely. But I think he clipped it.'

'Utter tripe,' said Terence. He threw his glass onto the ground, where it smashed.

'Gentlemen,' offered John.

'There're no gentlemen here,' said Terence. He lunged forward, swinging a punch towards Federico. Soon the two men were grappling, and Corey raced to pull them apart. As he pushed him away, John saw Stephen holding up a shotgun.

'He missed.'

The shotgun was pointed at Frederico. Corey looked over with angry eyes.

'That's not on. Put that down before somebody gets killed.'

'I think we should calm down, gentlemen,' said John. 'Put the gun down.'

'You need to tell the truth,' said Stephen, looking at Frederico.

'No,' said Frederico. 'The truth is told by that man,' he said, pointing at Corey.

Stephen looked at John. 'Did you miss?'

'I told you, it nearly took my shoulder off. I didn't see it, but you need to put the gun down.'

John wished Hope was here. She would have strolled in and taken command. His love was used to this sort of situation, for she'd even told him about the odd incident. You had to look like you were in charge; you had to look like you were the one who was in control.

John stepped forward and put his hand on the shotgun.

'Give me!' he said. 'Right now, right now before somebody gets killed.'

The man looked at him, and then he tutted, before handing over the gun. John stepped back with it, wondering what to do with the loaded weapon.

'You owe me money,' said Terence, pointing at Federico.

'And me,' said Stephen. The two of them turned and marched away. Federico turned around and threw his arms around John, the shotgun between the two of them.

'Easy,' said John.

'First shot and you hit it. I knew it. I knew you would. Wonderful man!' Federico walked over to the drinks and poured two large tumblers of whiskey and brought one back for John. John was still holding the shotgun and nodded at the drink, indicating it should be put down on the table.

Federico laughed, downed his drink in one go and then walked out of the shooting range.

'Well, that was interesting,' said Corey. 'Bit lively.'

'Can you take the gun?' asked John, holding it gingerly. 'If it's still loaded, I don't know what to do with it. Can you "de-load" it?'

'Uncock it, make it safe,' said Corey, laughing.

'Are they always like this?'

'Just because people invest money together doesn't mean there's a lot of love between them,' said Corey. 'Anyway, I've got quite an admiration of you going. She's quite the woman you've found. I had to pay for mine to come.'

'Pay?' blurted John.

'An escort. Good one though. Expensive. Keeps you warm though, if you know what I mean.'

Corey tapped John on the shoulder. He looked around at the guns that were left, made them safe and made his excuses, leaving the range. John was shaking, wondering what was going on. *What was this madhouse he'd come into? Absolute nutters*, he thought. *One hundred percent fruit loops.*

As he walked towards the door of the shooting range, his hands were shaking. *Twenty grand on me. Insanity!* he thought.

Chapter 09

Ian was finally satisfied, and Hope placed him down in the cot. She'd pick him up in a moment, but first she wanted to enjoy a bit of sea breeze. She pressed the button that opened up the large glass-fronted window, allowing it to slide up just a little, for outside was breezy. The wind was so strong that she couldn't even hear anything from the shooting range. Maybe it was just the angle. Hope was low down, and the shots were aimed away from them. She wasn't sure he would be, but she hoped John was having a good time.

Having taken in some of the sea breeze, she closed the window again, got the baby carrier and placed Ian in it. Then she left the pod, walked the pontoon back to the large lounge and sat down inside. She thought about getting a book, but she wasn't good at reading. She was better at watching. People-watching was a pastime for her, but then again, she was a detective.

Hope made her way over to the coffee machine and had a go at making herself a latte. As she did so, Ollie the chef came out. She went to smile at him, and to talk about how wonderful the croissants were, but the look he gave her was one of annoyance. She didn't push it any further, wondering if something was up with him. As he wandered back and forward, she caught him looking at her, almost gruffly, before he finally disappeared towards the staff quarters.

Hope thought about walking after him, to ask if he was okay, but Hamish appeared, smiling as ever.

'How's our little one today?' asked Hamish.

'He's fine, fast asleep, and his mother is just going to put her feet up. Thought I might even read for a bit. I was going to make one of the lattes. I've never made one before but Ollie seemed to be a bit, I don't know, occupied?'

'He is a bit occupied. He had a bit of a late-night last night, helping me, but, like I said, everything's good. All good with you?' asked Hamish.

'The place is amazing,' said Hope. 'I love the sound of the water outside. That big window, the way you're able to pull it back. It's quite something. I imagine in summer, if you get the weather right here, it'll be stunning. November's a little on the chilly side. That water's cold. I felt it when I went in the other day, and I was in a wetsuit.'

'Thank you again for that,' said Hamish. 'You're obviously quite a strong swimmer.'

'It's the sport I excel in,' said Hope. 'But it was the first time in since having this little guy. And well, to be honest, I was quite surprised I was still as strong. Everything changes when you have a wee one. Been finding that out.'

'I wouldn't know,' said Hamish, and smiled at little Ian.

'Terrible shame though for Ivor and Hannah and their kids to have to go. But you say he's still doing okay.'

'Well, I have heard nothing since I announced it earlier this morning. And I doubt I will. Still, at the end of the day, it's a private affair because it's his medical business. So, I'm not expecting any further updates. I know that they're not coming back because the doctor basically said he had to rest up for the next few days. And I think they'll head off somewhere else after that. One problem with these people is that, well, although they invested together, they don't always get on well. It's one thing to do business; it's another thing to actually be amongst each other, all used to being top dog.'

'Well, you'll get no arguments from me here,' said Hope. 'Just glad to be here.'

'And I'm delighted to have you,' said Hamish. 'It makes a change. Some of the rest of them are not the easiest to deal with. I'm getting paid to do it, and I shouldn't really say it, but I feel I can say it to you.'

'I'll not mention it,' said Hope. 'One thing struck me though,' she said. 'Last night when it all kicked off, how do you organise such a thing? How do you actually get people here? People were talking about a helicopter earlier on, specifically Laura. But she said she didn't hear a helicopter, so she was talking about a boat.'

Hamish laughed. 'A boat wouldn't be quick, would it?'

'But I didn't see any helipads when we arrived.'

'The thing about a helipad though, isn't it?' said Hamish. 'It's at the top.'

'But you never showed one on our tour.'

'No, because, to be quite honest, we don't want anybody going there. If you're going to use the helipads, you have to know what you're doing. Give the right signals for helos to come in. Make sure the pads is clear of FOD. Make sure that there's no fog on it. It's quite a specialist thing, and I don't want people, especially other people who are here, to think they know what they're doing. It leads to disaster.'

'FOD?'

'Foreign Object Debris. Can be catastrophic for a helicopter.'

'Well, I can understand that. It's just that Laura said she didn't hear any rotors in the night. She was up all night. I think the pair of them are, well, they're not newlyweds, but they seem to act like it.'

'She does indeed seem to be thrilled,' said Hamish. 'But she must have fallen asleep because there was a helicopter. I know, as I was there.'

'One of the big ones,' asked Hope.

'Coastguard. It's the Coastguard I have to talk to for medical advice. We're so far out here and I don't have a landline connected. I have a cell phone I can call through on but if you want to get evacuated out of here, it's only the Coastguard who can do it. The air ambulance helicopters find this quite a long run for their range, especially with the weather.'

'I thought they might just drop down a paramedic, you know?'

'You have a lot of experience of the rescue helicopter?' asked Hamish suddenly.

'A lot of experience? No, you see them on those programs though, don't you?' said Hope. 'They've got a winchman, and he comes out the bottom. Not seen much of it in real terms though.'

'Reality is quite different sometimes from the TV, but here, come with me.'

Hamish took Hope through down a corridor to the staff quarters. He passed a door on his left. 'I'll not take you in there,' he said. 'That's my quarters and the rest of the staff. Personal and private. You'll appreciate that.'

'Of course,' said Hope. 'I wouldn't want to disturb anyone.'

'In here on the right, that's our little medical suite.'

He opened the door, and Hope stepped inside. There was a little couch where you could be examined. There were several pills and different medical items stashed away in a cupboard, places for hands to be washed, and also a large laptop.

'That's where I link through to the doctors. I can also show them the patient via video link. People out here, they don't want to be disturbed. They don't want to go to a proper hospital if they can help it. You always have to have that backup though.' He took Hope back out of the medical room and further along the corridor.

'In here,' he said. 'These are our communications.' Hope looked at the dials in the room and various bits of equipment. 'That's the satellite phone,' he said. 'We also link up via satellite to the internet here. Besides that, we can call on Channel 16 for the coastguard or to any vessel around here.'

'And the coastguard can hear you all the way out here.'

'Big aerial,' he said.

'I didn't see an aerial when I arrived,' said Hope. 'The top of the structure looked flat.'

'Come with me,' said Hamish, laughing. He took Hope further down the corridor then out of a door, up some steps, and onto the roof of the facility. There, he pointed at a large H that had been painted.

'This square of roof is quite flat,' he said. 'If I want to, I can do this.' He pressed a button on a panel at the side, and small railings suddenly emerged, forming a low fence around the helicopter pad.

'They're not very high, but they let you know when you're going to disappear off the side. Otherwise, you don't come up here.'

He walked Hope out onto the middle of the pad. 'Over there,' he said, pointing to another part of the facility. 'Watch this.' He turned, went back to the control panel and pressed something. Suddenly, an aerial grew like a metallic magical beanstalk. It went up high, at least fifty feet up.

'That's amazing.'

'That's how we reach the Coastguard. They don't reach us. We reach them when we want to talk to them. If I keep that aerial up, I will have good communication. So, if something goes drastically wrong, we can talk to them from here. I hope that puts your mind at rest. We're medically equipped to handle any emergency. Got a defib here, too. I'm also, as they say, a good first medical option.'

'I am impressed. What about little babies, though? What if something was wrong with Ian?'

'Again, I can diagnose them from a basic standpoint, but I'd be straight on to the doctor. We don't just have one doctor we can go to. We can go to a paediatric doctor, we can go to a geriatric doctor, we can go to any type of doctor we want. All on call, all on standby, ready to pick up at a moment's notice.'

'It's quite impressive,' said Hope. However, she was looking at the helipad. If a Coastguard helicopter had landed here, she was surprised that she hadn't heard it, never mind Laura. Hope had been standing beside the landing site of one of the Sikorsky 92s when they landed. They were noisy, really noisy. Yes, she believed they could set down here. Yes, she believed the place was set up for them but she found it hard to believe that she hadn't heard them arrive last night.

'And they landed right here,' she said to Hamish. 'It's amazing. Didn't bother with a winch, just landed and came down.'

'Save some fuel,' said Hamish. 'Can you imagine it's a long

way out here? They don't want to spend any more time in the air than they have to. We haven't got fuel here for helicopters. So, they have to have enough when they land to go back again. So rather than come down and rush the assessment, if they land, their paramedic can take his time and make an unhurried decision.'

'I'm quite blown away,' said Hope. 'It's very impressive. Everything about this is impressive. It must be fun to work here.'

'I think it would be fun if everyone were like you,' said Hamish. 'Unfortunately, some of them are not. I should be professional, but it's difficult.'

'You don't really mean difficult, do you?' said Hope, laughing.

'Some of them can be right arses,' said Hamish. 'But I'm here to cater. They are my masters, and they pay me. So please, don't pass that on.'

'Of course I won't,' said Hope.

Hamish took her back down through the staff quarters and out back into the main lounge. As they arrived, Stephen and Terence burst through the door from the shooting range.

'It's too much.' Terence suddenly pointed at Hope. 'And your man just cost me twenty grand. Cost us both twenty.'

They stormed off towards their pods, leaving Hope in bemusement. Federico entered a few minutes later and marched up to Hope. He was going to throw his arms around her but then saw she was carrying Ian. He bent down and kissed the baby's head.

'Your man is wonderful. He can do anything. He can do anything. No wonder when he has such a beautiful woman behind him.'

Maisie Humphreys, Federico's wife, came from the pods.

'Stephen and Terence just banged on our pod. They were swearing at me. What's that about?'

'It is her husband.'

'He's not my husband,' said Hope. 'He's my partner.'

'Her man. He is wonderful, amazing. Made me forty grand. All with the shot. One shot. Never before has he held a gun, and he hits. He is special. But then he finds a special woman like this.'

'Stop ogling her. I'm sorry,' said Maisie. 'It's the trouble with them. They get drinking and they think we're here to be enjoyed, to be looked at.'

'But she is beautiful. Like you, my dear.' Federico walked over and suddenly waltzed with Maisie, kissing her on the cheek as he did so.

Corey came in and looked over at Hope. 'Your John is some guy; he's really set the cat amongst the pigeons.'

Hope was bemused, and then saw John coming in. Federico turned.

'Get that man a drink!'

'I've had enough to drink,' said John. He walked over towards Hope, who could smell the whisky on his breath.

'Enjoy yourself?' she asked.

'I've only had a couple. These guys, they're putting down tumblers worth,' he whispered. 'Federico's hammered.'

'I thought you were shooting.'

'Yes!' said John. 'I want coffee.'

'I'll make you one,' said Hope. She went over to look again at the coffee machine. Hope thought about what baristas did, and then suddenly Ollie was there, Hamish in the background. Ollie asked what Hope wanted. After ordering a couple of lattes, she turned back to John.

'It all kicked off up there,' he whispered. 'They were betting on whether I could hit a clay pigeon.'

'Did you?'

'I've no idea,' he said. 'It hurt my shoulder. Knocked me back when I fired, but I've no idea if I hit things or not. Corey said I nicked it.'

'Here,' said Frederico suddenly. He had a wad of cash, holding it out to John. 'Two thousand. For your trouble.'

'No,' said John. 'No, no. No, I can't take that.'

'You said you hadn't the money to bet. Take it and bet now.'

'Give it to charity,' said John. 'Give it away.'

'But you have nothing. You have so little in comparison. Spend it. Spend it on your beautiful wife.'

'We have everything,' said Hope, her arm around John, the other hand showing little Ian sleeping in the carrier.

Ollie came over with two lattes. 'And I have coffee,' said John. 'Coffee, Hope, and the wee man. I'm rich.'

'You're as cheesy as they come,' said Hope in his ear. But John was smiling. Whether that was the alcohol, or whether he was just made up, Hope wasn't totally sure.

Chapter 10

One window on the pod was lifted, but not by much. It allowed Hope to step outside and into the water. She swam close to the pod, enjoying the cold of the water, for a good five minutes before she got back out.

Watching from the bed was John. He'd been asleep when she got into the water, but now he was observing her, having recovered from his whiskies earlier on in the day. They had made him tired because he wasn't used to drinking at that time of the day.

'You're up. I thought the two men in my life were asleep,' said Hope, looking over at Ian in his cot. Of course, he would be up shortly. He slept a lot but then he would get up, look around the place, and want attention.

'You enjoying that?' asked John. 'Freezing, that water.'

Hope wrapped a towel around herself. 'It's brisk,' she said. 'But it's lovely. It's truly lovely.'

'One thing I won't understand about you. Doing that. Once was enough for me.'

'I'll get you in there with me.'

'You'll have to rescue me, no doubt,' said John, laughing.

'Shush,' said Hope. 'You'll wake him up.'

She tiptoed over to the cot, pulled the blanket back up over Ian, which he'd kicked off. She then closed the window of the pod and came and lay beside John on the bed, placing another towel underneath her to catch any drips.

'What happened up there then? I know they said you won twenty grand for them. In fact, some forty grand for him, but what went on with them?'

'You wouldn't believe it. They were betting on whether I'd hit this clay pigeon. I mean, I've never shot before. I told them that. Corey seemed to put a bit of sense to the proceedings, but there was a big ruckus over whether I'd hit it. It was coming to blows. I had to step in. At one point, somebody had a gun. It was . . . was it Terence? Anyway, the gun was actually loaded and pointing. I'm not sure he had any intention of firing it, but you don't do that with weapons.'

'No,' said Hope, 'you don't. You don't mess around them. And at a shooting range like that, I thought you'd have to take a lot more care.'

'There's nobody overseeing it. Don't you have some sort of range captain or something? Somebody who says, yes, you can, yes, you don't.'

'I guess with their money they do whatever they want,' said Hope.

'Well, it was darn risky. Didn't really enjoy it. And they were slamming the whiskies into them like anything. Big tumblers of it.'

'You're not used to that,' said Hope, laughing. She heard Ian start and rolled over, taking the child out of the cot. She went to bring him close to her, but she was cold, having been in the water, so handed him over to John. 'Let him cuddle up with you.'

'Well, he's going to want to feed in a minute. He always wants to eat when he wakes up.'

'Give me a minute,' said Hope. She went off to the shower and returned a few minutes later feeling a lot warmer, and took the child. She held him close until he motioned he wanted to eat. Hope let him lie close by John.

'They're pretty wild here. I thought coming away to all this decadence and stuff they'd be classier.'

'I think we're beyond the people who aim to be classier. I think these people think they just own everywhere. They seem to do what they want.'

'Hamish is struggling with them. He said so to me,' said Hope. 'Actually, he told me not to tell any of them, because technically they're his boss.'

'Well, as far as I see it,' said John, 'maybe we just stay aloof. Enjoy the place, what we can, and, yes, just enjoy each other before you go back.'

'They're not all like that, though,' said Hope. 'Laura's lovely, and I enjoy her company. Nice girl. She's besotted with that Paul now. Apparently, they were split up at one point, but they've got back together, and she's thinking he might propose to her.'

'Well, leave them well alone to do that,' said John. 'Don't put your nose in. You don't want to wreck anything.'

'What do you mean, wreck anything?'

'Well, you know what I mean. Just let them be.'

'I don't know,' said Hope. 'I'm still not convinced about Ivor and Hannah disappearing with their kids.'

'Well, they're not here, are they?' said John. 'I mean, clearly, they're not here, so they must have gone somewhere else. Your trouble is you see bodies everywhere. You'll be telling me next they dumped them off the back into the sea.'

'I hadn't thought of that one,' said Hope, and John flashed a look at her, only to see her smile.

'I don't mean that,' she said. 'Something's off. I've got that feeling.'

'Why do you get that feeling now?' moaned John. 'You don't need to have that feeling. Are you sure you haven't been able to have that feeling for a while? You've been away from it for so long, you're suddenly seeing everything. You're suddenly wanting there to be an issue for you to react. Give it two weeks, and you'll have plenty of time to go at it. Plenty of people; you'll have bodies everywhere.'

'The Highlands aren't quite like that,' said Hope.

John looked at her. 'How many cases?' he said brusquely.

Hope nodded. She had seen too many people die in her time. 'I just want to find out who they are to make sure there's nothing going on. I don't have the internet, I don't have Ross to ask about.'

'Alan. Why would you need Alan?'

'Alan Ross can go into any computer. He can dig everything about you out . All your history. It's what he does best.'

'I thought he was charging around with you now. Your sergeant, what you were to Macleod.'

'Alan's skills lie elsewhere, I'm beginning to think. But anyway, I haven't got him. So, I need to do it myself. No internet. I'm going to have to talk to them.'

'Well, don't go upsetting them. You're on holiday. Stop seeing issues. They're just a load of rich nutters. That's all.'

'I'll be careful.'

'Careful? What do you mean by careful? You don't have to be careful. Just don't upset them.'

'When he's finished here, I'm going to make us some dinner. I fancy making what I want tonight.'

'Really?'

'Yes, I do,' said Hope.

'You're not just going there so you can stand in the lounge and have something to do while you're observing everyone.'

'You said I have to take it easy and not be the detective.'

'I know what I've said,' John counted, 'but what that means is very little. The DI's on her case here. Hey, she's got it between the teeth. She's grabbed the bit. Here we go.'

'Stop it,' said Hope. 'Just let me have a word. It'll probably all blow over in the next couple of hours. I'll be satisfied, and then we can get on with the holiday. If I don't do this, I'm going to be thinking about it the whole time. And you said that I'm meant to be resting. I won't rest unless I—'

'Well, go off and do your detecting then. Okay,' said John. 'Promise me when you find out, that's it. For the rest of this holiday, you will chill out.'

'I promise,' said Hope. She reached over and kissed him. It was another five minutes before she took Ian off the breast and handed him to his dad. 'You wind him,' said Hope. 'I'll go make that dinner.' As she rolled off the bed, she heard that familiar sound. Ian had just exploded in his nappy.

'Timing. That's what I call that,' said John. 'Timing.'

Hope pulled on some tracksuit bottoms and her T-shirt before following the pontoon into the lounge area. She moved over to the kitchen side, looking at what to make for dinner that night. She pulled out some rice, put it on to boil, and found some chicken in the fridge. Carefully, she chopped it to put it into a pan, found some onions, and some seasoning. It would be a basic dinner, but it would be good enough. As she stood watching it cook, Laura came up behind her.

'Paul's busy working on something, so I thought I'd get out of the way. He could be a while, so I'm going to make myself something.'

'Trouble?' asked Hope.

'No, no, he's just one of those people who, when he thinks of something, has to sit down and work on it. So, I've got out of the pod. Get out of the way. It's the way he is, intensely focused. He seems able to switch himself off to just about everything except what he's focused on.'

'You're welcome to join me,' said Hope. 'I'm just making something for us. I'm kind of tired of having somebody else make it.'

'Well, I never tire, but, oh well, I'll join you.'

Laura went to find some pasta, grabbed a saucepan, and pulled out some pre-made sauces.

'How well do you know all these people?' asked Hope.

'Well, I know most of them from Paul, and he has told me about some of them.'

'Well, Ivor, for instance—who is he?'

'Well, Paul knows him because he's a British CEO. He works for a construction company in South America. Paul himself is a Scottish CEO. He runs a logistics firm. They said it's trailblazing. At least, that's what the magazine said. But he works worldwide. He met these guys in Brazil.'

'But then there was all the fighting earlier on today up at the range. Who are those people then? I mean, I know I've met them, and I know what they said they were.'

'Well, Steve Winters has a tech company. And it's a big one. It sits above lots of other tech companies. He's American, as you've heard.'

'Why was he agitated then? Can't he afford to lose twenty thousand?'

'They can afford to lose it,' said Laura, 'but they don't like to lose. And that's the thing; it's not the money. Twenty thousand to these guys, they can afford to lose that easily, and often do.'

'Did you grow up with this sort of lifestyle?' asked Hope.

'No,' said Laura. 'Paul found me. I was working at a club.'

'What sort of club?'

'No, not like that. I was serving behind the bar, and he chatted me up. We got to know each other, and that's where it started . He showed me a completely different lifestyle.'

'Were you down in Brazil with him?'

'No, he just talked about it. Federico and Terence, though, I know they've both got different energy companies. They're CEOs and at each other's throats over a lot of things. But both their firms were working down in Brazil with Paul. I don't know why, but he came up with this idea of a place.'

'I didn't understand that bit. Why would you create this out here? It is unique but even so.'

'Getting away from it all is difficult,' said Laura, 'for these people. They get hounded. The press hounds them. You can't get hounded out here. Go to somewhere like the Maldives and the press will get there easily. You approach here, and we will know about it.'

'And they bought it all together, did they?' asked Hope.

'Paul said they just got talking one night, and this is what they came up with. They put the money in, and it got built.'

'But they don't seem to like each other. I mean, how is Federico involved if Terence hates him so much?'

'It's the investment. Things get put aside sometimes when investments are made. They're looking to hire this out to other people with serious money.'

'Well, I can see why people would come. Quite a thing, isn't it? But it's also quite simple. I mean, I don't get it. Why wouldn't you just want to go somewhere with a lot of staff, a lot of attention for you? You could have security around the grounds to make sure nobody comes in. You could—'

'You don't get it, do you?' said Laura. 'Certainly with Paul, they like the solitude. They like the quiet. They enjoy being away from everything.'

'I think I'd be happy just going to a little hut somewhere,' said Hope.

'But you can,' said Laura. 'Paul couldn't. Too many people could find him. Too many people could annoy him. They can't do that here.'

'There's no proper security here, is there?' said Hope. 'Given how you describe it, do they have conflict in the work they do?'

'Paul says somebody's always unhappy, whatever you do, despite being given environmental awards. I mean, that's the thing. They were involved in something good down there in Brazil. They put it all together, but somebody always complains about it. I was with Paul at a restaurant in England, and this guy just came up and threw water over Paul. Said he deserved a lot more on him. And said it should sweep him away. I asked Paul about that, but he didn't really say anything. He just said not to worry. It was just one of these nutters. Anyway, they must have been doing a good thing down in Brazil because after all, they got an award for it, and a conservation one. I mean, they don't hand those out willy-nilly, do they? Especially to big companies.'

'Suppose not,' said Hope. Hope looked up and saw a woman

walking in with a younger woman beside her.

'I don't know who that is, though,' said Hope, 'I've seen her about.'

'Alison Mathers, and that's Emily, her daughter. I don't know them. Apparently she's the chief executive of a recruitment company. Again, worked with Paul down in South America, he said.'

Behind them, Corey appeared, along with a woman.

'And who's that with Corey? I know he's a . . . what?'

'An American official working down in South America. I guess Corey's a mover and shaker. The woman with him, however, Paul said she's . . . well, I shouldn't say what he said.'

'Why, what did he say?'

'I would say escort. He said hooker.'

'You're telling me Corey can't get himself a woman?' asked Hope. 'With all his money, he should have somebody hanging off him.'

'Oh, I don't know what he's like,' said Laura. 'I mean, we don't all go after them just because of their money.'

'Oh, sorry,' said Hope. 'I didn't mean it that way. And anyway, Paul came back for you, didn't he?'

'Yes, he did. It's okay. No offence taken. I know you didn't mean it that way.'

'I really didn't,' said Hope. 'I'm sorry if I offended. It's just funny. I've been here for several days, and I don't know everybody.' She looked over at the woman with Corey. 'What's her name?'

'Well, she's calling herself Sylvia, but Paul says that won't be her real name.'

'She's very good-looking,' said Hope.

'Well, Paul says that's because Corey paid good money. You

pay enough money; you can get a good-looking one.'

'We'd better get back to this dinner. It's nearly ready. Can you just keep an eye on it,' said Hope, 'and I'll get my boys.'

'Will do,' said Laura.

Chapter 11

Hope sat at the table, rice and chicken in front of her, with John sitting with Ian by her side. He was tucking into his dinner, in between Ian trying to pull at his face and grab hold of the fork. Hope was quite taken with what was going on. She loved seeing John with her wee boy. It was something that caught her out. She never expected it would be something that would feel so warm to her, so wholesome. She could sit and watch them forever.

Beside her, Laura was tucking into her pasta. The girl was chatty as ever, but Hope's eyes were everywhere else, watching, monitoring the guests. Many of them had passed their requests for dinner on to Ollie, and the food was being served to them. It wasn't a formal occasion like it had been the previous night, but the class of food coming out was just as wonderful. At least in Hope's eyes.

'That's Sylvia's enjoying it, isn't she?' said Laura.

'What do you mean?' asked Hope.

'The food. She's tucking into it rightly.'

'Well, she's probably not used to it, a bit like me. That's why I wanted something plainer tonight.'

'Sure, Ollie would have made you something plainer.'

'Cooking for my boys, though,' said Hope. 'It's quite something when you see them eating it. It's quite something to watch my man. Do you never cook for Paul?'

'Paul's always taking me out here and there.'

'Do you not get to have a say? Decide what you are going to do?'

'Paul generally decides. Takes us here and there. I mean, he's always got me going places. Theatres, some music recitals. He's not shy about taking me places. Likes me on his arm. Certainly, likes to be seen with me.'

'I suppose that's good,' said Hope. 'Bad if it was the other way.'

'Indeed,' said Laura.

'Well, that was a bit underwhelming,' said Hope. 'You all right?'

'When we were apart, when we split up that time, he had lots of different women on his arm. I know. I followed him. But now he's, well, he's got me again.'

'Hope he doesn't treat you like you're some sort of possession,' said Hope.

'Hope,' said John, 'it's not what we ask friends.'

'Oh, sorry,' said Hope. 'I didn't mean to.'

'You really just say as it is, don't you?' said Laura. 'I don't think so. I don't think he's like that with me. He just likes to spoil me, likes to see me in good things. Oh, here he is.'

Paul entered the lounge, looked over and smiled at Laura, and then went and sat at a separate table. Hope watched Laura's face. After he'd sat down, about a minute later, Ollie came out with a dish and placed it in front of Paul. The man picked up his fork and ate, but before long, he'd stopped.

'Laura,' he said across the tables, 'get the chef for me, will you?'

'Of course,' said Laura. And off she went. Hope found this strange. If John had said that to her, she'd have told him to see him himself. Regardless, Laura came back in followed shortly afterwards by Ollie, the chef.

'Do you understand what dish this is?' said Paul.

The chef looked at him and gave a little shake of the head, not to say he didn't know what the dish was, but more to say that he didn't understand what the problem was.

'Carnaroli rice, it should be with Carnaroli rice. This is the wrong rice. What rice is this? It should be Carnaroli rice!'

The chef shook his head for a moment and simply stood there.

'Are you mute? Are you dumb? What is wrong with you? We paid for a proper chef here. This is not Carnaroli rice. Look at it.'

Paul lifted the bowl and put it underneath Ollie's nose. Ollie brushed it away with his hand, and the dish nearly spilt. But Paul forced the dish back under his nose.

'Carnaroli rice. Any decent chef would know that this is made with Carnaroli rice. We'd pay damn good money to get you here. You should at least know what you're doing.'

The chef turned on his heel, but Paul shouted after him. 'Don't you walk away. I don't pay you money to walk away. I pay you money to explain yourself. Stand here, boy!' shouted Paul. 'Come here.'

Olly seemed to take exception to the term boy. He spun on his heel, walked right up to the table and put his face in front of Paul's. He started shouting in a foreign language.

'Don't you come on to me like that. I pay your wages. You'll take from me what I give you. Okay? Now stand there and shut up.' For a moment, Olly went silent. 'This is the wrong rice. Any monkey can make this dish.' Paul reached up and grabbed Olly's cheeks and pulled them. 'Oi, sunshine, sort yourself out. Make me a proper dish. I want the Carnaroli rice. I know it's here. He specifically said it would be here.'

As he let go of the cheeks, Olly reached down and grabbed the dish. At first, it looked like he would take it away with him, but instead, he picked it up and turned the bowl upside down. The rice, which was not Carnaroli rice, landed on top of Paul's head. Ollie let the dish go, and it smashed on the floor, approximately a table's distance away. He turned to go, but Paul jumped up, covered in the rice, and grabbed the man from behind. The sound of the crash had brought Hamish running into the lounge.

'What's going on?' he said.

Ollie was shouting in a foreign language that Hope couldn't make out. He was probably swearing because it looked like that's what he was doing. He was pointing at Paul at the same time as Paul was grabbing him by the throat.

'Stop it,' said Hamish. 'Enough. Enough, everyone.'

But Paul wasn't listening. Instead, he was throttling the chef. He was swinging his fist to strike the man.

Hope stood up, and she could tell John was looking at her with livid eyes.

'We'll have less of that,' said Hope. 'Everyone, stand down. Put some distance between you.'

'Shut up, tourist,' said Paul. 'We don't need some redheaded bimbo. I've got this under control.'

At this point, he took a swing, looking to punch Ollie in the face. Paul was startled when Hope caught him by the wrist and then drove it up behind his back. He yelled, letting go of the chef, who scurried away still shouting in a foreign language.

'I said enough,' said Hope. 'And I'm not a bimbo.'

She let go of Paul's wrist, and he turned to face her. She could see his own fists were pulled together and his arm started to go back as if he was going to let loose on her.

'I wouldn't,' said Hope. 'I really wouldn't.' The man reached back to take a swing. Hope ducked down and swept her leg around, taking the man's feet from under him. He fell straight onto his back. Hope then stood over him. 'I said it's enough. Don't even think of it.'

Paul got to his feet, staring at Hope with eyes like daggers, glanced over at Laura and then stormed off.

'Wow!' shouted Terence.

'I told you,' said Frederico. 'I told you, John, he picks wisely. John knows his women!'

Hope turned and stared at the men. 'I think we can all just go back to our meals.' Slowly she turned and walked back but was intercepted by Hamish.

'Thank you,' he said. 'Thank you.'

'Is Ollie okay?'

'Ollie is fine. These people. I keep telling you, these people.'

'It's all right. All done,' said Hope.

'Where did you learn to do that?'

'Just because I'm a mother doesn't mean I can't go to the gym and classes,' said Hope.

Hamish smiled. 'Well, I'm glad you did. Can we get you anything?'

'I'm fine. Let's all just get back to normal,' said Hope. She sat down, and Laura turned to her.

'Look, I'm so sorry,' she said. 'I'm so sorry. I don't know why he's doing that. Maybe he's under stress. Maybe he's—'

'It's fine,' said Hope.

'But he went to hit you.'

'He could have tried to hit me as much as he wanted. It wouldn't have worked.' She heard a cough from John.

'Let me get you a glass of water,' said Laura.

'That would be good,' said Hope, and let the woman disappear over to the water fountain. As she did so, John leaned into Hope's ear.

'Nice going. Definitely a mother. Not some sort of kick-ass detective then.'

'Point taken, but that was getting out of hand.'

'Indeed,' said John. 'I could have stood up and got involved.'

'You would have got your arse kicked,' said Hope.

'But you wouldn't have looked like some have-a-go hero who knows what she's doing. You'd have looked like the little housewife, not interfering, looking afraid.'

'I don't want to look afraid.'

'You're wanting to find out about these people. Don't antagonise them to their faces. You'll never find out what they're like. Be cooler and calmer.'

'What would you know about it?' said Hope suddenly.

John grinned. 'If you'd worked in a car hire firm and taken the crap I had to take for most of my life, you would have learned how to deal with customers while sounding professional and intelligent, while all the time wanting to punch them in the face.'

'Point taken,' said Hope. 'But you were holding Ian as well.'

'I am capable of passing my son over. Anyway, Laura's coming back.'

Laura set a glass of water in front of Hope. Hope, although she didn't really want it, drank it. She picked again at the rice in front of her.

'I wonder what Ollie was on about. He doesn't speak much English, does he?'

'No, he's speaking Portuguese,' said Laura. 'I have a little bit of it, not a lot, but that was definitely Brazilian Portuguese. Some words, I got .'

'When did you learn Brazilian Portuguese?'

'I spent some time down there, and I thought it would be wise to learn the language when I was down with Paul. I learned a bit, but you can pick it up easily. It's definitely a distinct sound from normal Portuguese. But like I said, I don't know everything. I'm behind on being able to interpret it straight away. I hope Paul's calmed down now.'

'Are you going to be all right with him?'

'Oh, he wouldn't hurt me,' said Laura. 'He might be angry and that, but if he's still like that, I'll come back and read a book or do something else. I know when to give him a wide berth. I guess that's good. When you get together in life, you have to understand each other, don't you?'

'That you do,' said Hope but she was staring towards John. He'd been right. Hope now had provided a rescue out at sea. She had stood up, all six feet of her, and broken up two men. The little housewife. She wasn't playing the part that well, not wanting anybody to know what she did for a living. John was perhaps more subtle.

'What was Brazil like?' asked Hope. As she sat and listened for the next half an hour, Laura told her about all the different places she'd seen in Brazil, but Hope wasn't getting what she needed. Hope had wanted to know about the work that Paul was doing, but Laura didn't seem to know. Every time Hope put a question that way, Laura would talk about something else.

The colours, the vibrancy of the land, the fresh fruits you could get there, how sometimes they needed escorting, but she hadn't understood why. The escorts weren't the same as British escorts. She talked about the clothing, the differences with the Brazilians, what they considered being decent and what not; how when they wore next to nothing that was decent, but as soon as you uncovered a breast, that was suddenly indecent. Laura struggled to see the difference as she thought just about everything was on show beforehand.

She raved about the culture, clearly being someone who'd enjoyed it when she was down there. After a while, Hope had heard enough. She had spent enough time talking and interviewing people to know when they knew something of use or not. She felt bad, but she used Ian as an excuse again.

'I'm afraid I'm going to have to go back and lie down with this little man,' she said to Laura.

'If you want to stay, I can do it,' said John. He received a kick under the table for that one.

'I think he might need his mum soon.'

Hope picked up Ian and, accompanied by John, made her way back to the pod. Once inside, she put Ian down on the bed and turned to John.

'Sorry, you're right. Of course you're right; I shouldn't have jumped up. I'll try not to be the detective.'

'I just wish you'd get over this. This thing about something being wrong.'

'No sound of a helicopter,' said Hope, 'doesn't feel right. Hamish is the one feeding us all the information about Hannah and Ivor, but he was the one who took them out of the picture. He was the one who spoke to them after everybody saw them disappear into the staff quarters. Nobody else saw them leave. Nobody else saw him fully recovered, or at least in a place to be transported.'

'And you're telling me if you'd heard the helicopter blades, you'd have been satisfied.'

'They were all together. They've all been in Brazil. Our chef speaks Portuguese, Brazilian,' said Hope.

'You think they hired him from down there. From Brazil?'

'They got a Michelin star chef; that's what they said about him. It's a Michelin star chef who didn't know that he needed Carnaroli rice?'

'Well, I didn't know you needed Carnaroli rice,' said John.

'I didn't either,' said Hope, 'but our chef should have. That's what Paul was angry about it. I'm just finding . . . well, I've got that feeling.'

'I'm just going to have to let you get your head on this, aren't I?' said John. 'Let you explore and come to an answer.'

'You are,' said Hope.

'Just one thing,' said John, and he wrapped his arms around her waist and pulled her in close. He kissed her on the side of the neck, then under the ear, and then whispered, 'You looked great tonight sorting them out.'

Hope could feel John's arms around her as she lay wistfully dozing on the bed. She'd been up in the middle of the night because Ian had decided he wasn't quite comfortable or something. Having got him back to sleep, Hope had then wrapped herself up in the arms of her partner, hoping not to be disturbed that morning. However, the bell on their pod went just a little after eight.

'Who the hell's that?' asked John.

'Would you find out?' pleaded Hope.

She felt a kiss on the back of her neck before John got out of bed and put on a dressing gown. John went to the pod door. When the door opened, she glanced the dress of a woman. Hope then heard Laura.

'I was hoping to speak to Hope if she's awake. I just feel terrible about last night.'

'Hope's fine,' said John. 'Just give me a second.'

John turned around and looked over towards the bed where Hope nodded and then rolled out of the far side of the bed. She put a dressing gown on and walked over to the door of the pod, where Laura was looking sheepish.

'Did I wake you? I'm sorry,' she said. 'Didn't mean to. I

hoped maybe we could go out for a swim or something this morning.'

'A swim,' said Hope.

'You like swimming, don't you? I guess I just wanted to say sorry for Paul's behaviour.'

'Was he all right with you last night?' asked Hope.

'I kind of broached it with him and, well, to be fair, no, he wasn't. He was a bit off.'

'He didn't hit you?' asked Hope.

'No, no. No, nothing like that. He was still angry. Still angry this morning. So, I was just getting out of the way. Can we go for a swim?'

'Of course we can,' said Hope. And then she turned to look back at John. 'I can go for a swim, can't I?'

'It's not me you need to be looking at,' said John. 'It's that wee guy.'

'He'll need feeling in a bit when he wakes up, but yes we can go for a swim, can we say an hour?'

'Okay,' said Laura, 'where will I meet you?'

'Well, they have that snorkelling gear, don't they, down towards the harbour? We'll go down there and get some wetsuits on, and go for a proper swim, a long one. I just need to make sure this boy's fed; otherwise, John won't be able to keep him quiet. Sometimes he needs his mum.'

'Of course,' said Laura. 'I'll see you in a bit.'

The door of the pod closed, and Hope turned around and looked at John. 'What do you make of that?'

'Well, she's either trying to find a way to apologise, or she's scared herself, and she's keeping out of her partner's way. After all, you've shown you can handle him.'

'True,' said Hope. 'I pray it's not the second one. Maybe she's just trying to make up to me. She doesn't need to. She did nothing.'

'No,' said John, 'but she'll feel responsible.'

It was another half hour before Ian woke up. And by the time Hope had fed him, and then got herself down to the harbour, Laura had been waiting over an hour.

'I apologise,' she said. 'It's him, the wee man. The wee man does what the wee man wants. He has breakfast when he wants to have breakfast, not when I decide he has breakfast.'

'Oh, it's my fault. I called you too early,' said Laura.

They disappeared inside the small changing cubicles, put on full wetsuits, and came out in snorkels and flippers. Entering the water, Hope could see that Laura was looking much happier. They tied their hair up, put the goggles with the snorkels on, and swam in the water.

It wasn't like swimming back off the coast of Scotland. Hope didn't feel there was as much to see here, and she didn't want to stray too far in the water. So they swam around the edge of the structure. They saw some of the men out fishing in the rowing boat. Terence was one of them. When he saw the red hair of Hope passing by, he shouted out to her.

'There's our girl. There's the one that can handle him.'

Hope gave a sarcastic wave. As they were only about twenty yards away from the boat, it didn't take long when an argument surfaced for the women to hear it. There was shouting, a commotion. Hope thought there might even be fisticuffs. But she didn't care.

If they went in this time, they'd just have to sort themselves out. It sounded cold, and she wasn't sure she'd actually achieve her dispassion, if it came to it. Instead, she swam away, and after checking with Laura that she was competent to swim underneath the structure, the two women went below.

The amount of pipework under the structure was incredible, and Hope was fascinated by what she saw. She was no mechanical engineer and did not understand how it was built, but she found it intriguing to swim amongst the stanchions. She surfaced on the other side.

When she looked around, she suddenly realised that she was at the rear, where the boat had docked, close to the quarters of the staff. Along one pontoon sitting at the end, both smoking, were the two cleaners, Ella and Geordie. They were talking in a language she didn't understand, but Laura swam up beside her. She went to speak, but Hope put her hand over her mouth.

'Say nothing,' she whispered. 'I don't want to disturb them. This is their area. They don't want to think people are here. We should go back.'

Hope went to turn away, but Laura put a finger up to her mouth, telling Hope to shush. Hope watched the woman concentrating so hard for the next few minutes. Then when the cleaners suddenly stood up, extinguishing their cigarettes, Laura put her mask on and instantly dropped beneath the surface.

Hope followed her. Laura was swimming back, away from the docking area, back towards the pods at the front of the structure. They swam around to the front, and Laura stopped at Hope's pod. She held on tightly at the front of it as Hope came up beside her.

'You all right?'

'I am,' said Laura but she was clearly thinking about something. 'Shall we get a shower?' said Hope. 'Get back out of these. Then we could go up to the lounge.'

'Can we get in here?' she said.

'Why?' asked Hope.

'I want to keep out of Paul's way at the moment. If I go back to the pod, he might be there. If I go through to the lounge, he might be there.'

'You wait here then,' said Hope. 'I'll get out at the harbour. I'll walk through, and I'll open up our window here in the pod. I'll make sure John's not in. You can shower and change here if you want. Are your clothes back up at the harbour?'

'Yes,' she said.

It took Hope about five minutes before she was opening the front window of the pod and allowing Laura to climb in. Hope let the woman use the shower first. By the time Hope had used it and changed, Laura was sitting looking out the bay window in the clothes Hope had brought back for her.

'Are you okay?' asked Hope.

'It's just something I heard,' said Laura.

'From whom? From those cleaners?'

'Yes, they were speaking Portuguese, Brazilian Portuguese, but the dialect was thick. I found it hard to understand.'

'But you must have heard something,' said Hope, 'because it's affected you.'

'It looks like he messed up. Ivor got milk in one of his meals.'

'Okay, so Ollie screwed up, Ivor had a reaction, and now he's off to hospital,' said Hope. 'No harm done in the long run. I guess they just want to keep that covered up.'

'Well, that's maybe true, but something they said, "it didn't matter." I think I'm translating this correctly. "It didn't matter, as the man wouldn't have long, anyway." What does that mean?'

'I don't know. Were they talking about Ollie? Maybe Ollie's getting the boot. I mean, he had that to-do with Paul, and Paul was right about the rice, wasn't he?'

'I wouldn't have a clue,' said Laura, 'but he's usually right about those things.'

'You look a bit shaken, though. Can I get you a drink or something?'

'Yes, let's have a drink,' said Laura. Hope pressed a button and the pod window moved back. It was a strong breeze, but it was a good one, and Hope sat down beside Laura.

'I hope I'm doing the right thing,' she said. 'Seeing him react like that, when he went to hit you, I just—'

'Don't worry about it. I wouldn't have been in any danger.'

'Why?' asked Laura, and Hope realised she'd wandered into the situation again.

'I'm trained. Martial arts. Comes with the job. I don't like to tell people, but I'm good at self-defence.'

'It worries me I might need self-defence, though,' said Laura. 'Paul's so like that. So direct, you know. Scares me sometimes. And yet he's so good to me, unlike the others. I don't feel like an object. Not like Sylvia. I'm not bought to be here.'

'But you're not like the others yet either, are you?'

'Their partnerships. You see the women with their men. They're in it together.'

'Maybe they've just had longer,' said Hope. 'It takes time. John and I have been together for a little while now. We're different now from when we began. We complement each other better than we ever did. He knows me. He's able to say things.'

'But he's such an affable guy.'

'That he is,' said Hope.

'He also goes out and earns the bread for you. He doesn't expect you to work. Paul will expect me to do something. I won't just be his kept lady. He'd want me to be a professional of some sort. He'd like to tell people that.'

Hope sat thinking about what John had sacrificed to let her have her career. Or her calling, as she would put it. It wasn't a career. It was a calling. She was like Seoras. She couldn't not be a detective. Even here, she was being a detective. Even here, he was letting her run around. She was blessed, she thought. Truly blessed.

She had a mentor who helped her develop, helped her become the detective she was. She had a partner now who was going to let her do that. And she had a little one to come home to, someone for the both of them to share.

'If you need anything,' Hope said to Laura, 'you come to me. If he in any way reacts violently or mistreats you, you come to me.'

'He'll have lawyers. He would figure a way out of things if he ever did anything like that,' said Laura. 'But I don't think he will. I'm going to marry him when he proposes. I'm sure he's going to propose. He needs to calm down first, though.'

'Does he often get annoyed like that?'

'He doesn't like it when things don't work out right,' said Laura. 'That should have been the right meal for him. He put things in place. The rice was meant to be here. It was ordered. I mean, that's all he was talking about last time. Oh, last night when I went in, I tried to calm him, you know. I tried to sit and rub his shoulders. I tried to, well, I tried to talk him into bed to see me, to be together, to ease the pain in that way we do. But he wasn't having it. I guess I felt rejected in that sense. Something I should be able to do for him. Something I should be able to manage.'

'If he's dumb enough to brood over rice,' said Hope, 'while you're there in his room with him, and in an amorous mood, well, he's an idiot. Look at you, girl. You should be worth everything to him.'

'Thank you,' said Laura. 'You're quite something, you know that?'

She reached over and hugged Hope. Hope felt like she was the older sister. However, she knew also that something was bothering her. The cleaning staff had said it didn't matter as the man wouldn't have long, anyway. Had they meant Ollie for making the mistake of putting milk in? Or had they meant Ivor? Had they meant that Ivor would be dead soon?

She had no evidence. She needed the background and the background was so flimsy. All she had was Laura's knowledge of it. He owns this; they own that; they've all been in Brazil together. She had no details, nothing to understand. No connections to chew on. Oh, she wished Ross were here. With a laptop he'd get to the bottom of it in no time.

Chapter 13

John put on the baby carrier around his shoulders, popped in little Ian, and prepared to go for a walk since Hope was out with her friend. He had decided he just needed some time away. *The people here were nuts. High-powered, egotistical idiots*, John thought. The commotion that went on. He'd seen it all, of course. On a slightly different level.

People complaining about hire cars. People who complained about being hit by other cars while driving the hire car as if it was the company's fault for having given them the hire car in the first place. As the front face of the hire company, he had seen the bad side of human nature often. There were plenty of good times though, something he had to remind himself of.

The people who were delighted with the service, the people who thanked you and those who generally just got on with the daily banter of life. He'd had a good team, and the business had done well, but this was a new life, a different part of his life.

Hope wouldn't cope with being at home, even with little Ian to look after. Her mind is too active, John thought. She was dynamic in a way that John wasn't. She liked to take charge, to sort things out. John was much easier-going in a sense, and yet she was probably the one who would push for more fun things to do while relaxing.

He laughed at her idea of skinny dipping out in front of the pod. That was so Hope. There wouldn't be a crowd around, just him and her. Although she was no show-off, she had a cheeky side to her—one that they probably never saw when she had the ponytail up, being a detective. That was fine with John. There had to be a bit of her he kept for himself. A part not everybody else got to see.

John left the main structure, Ian in the baby carrier, and climbed up the grassy side of Boreray. 'It's quite something to be out here,' he said out loud as he wandered the newly constructed path up towards the top. He wouldn't go into the shooting range, although he couldn't hear any gunfire. Maybe they had decided not to threaten each other with guns today. Still, he couldn't believe the sheer recklessness of the way they treated the firearms. Well, he wouldn't be taking aim at any of that.

As he walked up, he stopped and stared out to sea. He could make out Hirta across the water, but after that, there was nothing. Absolutely nothing for miles. You were so far out here. He was fortunate today because it was a light wind, but he wondered what it would be like stuck here for two weeks if there was a hoolie going on.

If it was solitude you were looking for, though, this was a winner; except you'd have to make sure the people coming with you weren't, well, idiots like this lot. People who would be a bit more respectful of each other, because these people certainly weren't. They'd been ruined by money, or were they always like that? John didn't know.

He'd never been privileged in life to have that sort of money, but Hope had been so excited when he'd won the prize. And in truth, it was a lot of fun in the pod. They were getting time together, a more relaxing time together.

When Ian was born, it was rough going, because he was a baby and needed Hope all the time. John did his bit, as much as he could, winding him, carrying him around to get him back to sleep. But it had been good, and John thought it had brought Hope and him even closer together.

As he looked out across the sea, he could see something flying. It was a small plane. As it got closer, he recognised the colour scheme, for he'd seen it land once at Inverness Airport, and had a word with someone about it. It was a fishery protection plane. Apparently, they flew very low level, seeing who was fishing in the wrong place. In a strange way, it gave John some comfort. There was still something out there, more than this. They were still contactable, reachable.

'You not got that gorgeous wife with you?'

John turned and saw Corey Denman and his partner, Sylvia.

'Hope's off with Laura, having a swim. I'm just taking the little man out here. And she's not my wife. She's my partner.'

'Couldn't get her down the aisle then,' said Corey. 'Ah, it doesn't matter, anyway. Stuck with you once you've put one in the oven.'

John wanted to walk away, but he was far too polite. His years in the service industry made him produce a response that was honest but tactful.

'This little guy certainly helped us,' he said. 'But we were committed well before that.'

'What do you do anyway?' asked Corey sharply.

'Well, I used to run a car hire firm,' said John. He was about to say he was going to be a house dad, but then he remembered

Hope didn't want anyone to know about her being a police officer. So, he quickly said, 'I'm looking at options for what I do beyond that.'

Corey almost snorted. 'Well, I'm managing contracts for the US and Brazil. Mining down there has helped US firms, as well as some of the British ones. I've been instrumental in negotiating deals, getting the locals on board. Quite a place down there, a lot warmer than this. Made some good money out of it too, which is why I could buy into here. Done a good job here, too. You're very lucky getting to have a go here. After these couple of weeks, they're going to be paying through the nose for it. You're going to be talking movie stars. All the people who need to get away from the press. I'm sure you wouldn't understand that.'

John thought about how Hope would love to be away from the press in the middle of a murder investigation, but he said nothing.

'Oh look,' said Corey, 'it's Alison.' And he turned without even saying goodbye and marched off down the path, leaving Sylvia standing. John thought Sylvia would go with him, but she stayed and was looking directly at John's chest.

'Can I see him?' she asked.

The woman was quite tall, not quite at Hope's six feet, but getting there. With long blonde hair, she had a body that clearly worked out, for she was toned, and was wearing extremely tight clothing. There was a cleavage that leapt out at you, and John almost pitied the woman, for these were obviously her working clothes.

'Of course you can,' said John. He pulled the baby carrier to one side so that Ian's face could be seen.

'He's beautiful,' she said. 'You're so lucky.'

'I know,' said John.

'Did you give up your work when this one came along?'

'Yes.'

'You did that for her? That's amazing,' said Sylvia. She put her hand up on John's shoulder. 'I look at all the, well, idiots here, Corey included,' she said, 'and it's nice to find a decent man amongst them.'

John went a little red.

'You know what I do, don't you?' she said.

'You're a companion for hire,' said John. 'Is that the term?'

'Big money prostitute, more like,' said Sylvia and then gave a hollow laugh. 'I've got lots of gambling debts. I need to clear them. With people that, well, you don't not pay it back to.'

'Sorry to hear that,' said John.

'I'd love a wee one. I really would.'

'Forgive me for saying,' said John, 'but how do you not find a decent man? Look at you. I mean, you look great. I assume you're—'

'Don't look at me now,' she said. 'I was on drugs. That's where I racked up the bills. I've got myself off them, and that's a fight because these guys, you don't know what they're going to get you into.'

'Don't you need to be getting after him if he's paying you?' asked John.

'No, he's away. Alison's a favourite of his, and Corey actually likes Emily, Alison's younger one. That's the thing. When they can pick and choose, when they can pay, they treat you like you're just this object. He treats them like objects too, because he thinks all women are now like this.'

John sat down on the grass, and Sylvia sat beside him. 'It's a shame,' said John, 'it'd be great to help you. What are you anyway, twenty-five?'

'Twenty-two,' said Sylvia. John swallowed. It was wrong. He felt it was so wrong.

'I take it the sort of money we're talking about isn't a loan you could get from someone who ran a car hire firm.'

'No,' said Sylvia. 'You know what the biggest problem is? You sometimes see it dressed up, you know? In movies and that. And he's just a lonely guy who needs a companion. I'm meat to this guy. Corey is a drag. All he ever talks about is himself. When he talks to me, all he ever wants is, well, you know what he wants. And when he's not wanting that himself, he wants to show me off to the others to say, "look what I can buy." It sucks.'

'It certainly does,' said John.

'Do you mind if I take him? To hold him for a bit.'

John carefully took Ian out and handed him over to Sylvia. He had to show her how to hold him properly, because clearly, she had no experience. Once he was snuggled there in her arms, head lying on her chest, he gurgled. John saw Sylvia light up.

'This is something, isn't it?' she said. 'Bet you love this.'

'Course I do,' said John.

'Last night,' said Sylvia, 'after, well, he'd done the business— which wasn't long, thank God—he went on and on to me about how he organised a takeover of an entire area of Brazil. He had to move out the indigenous tribe. But some stayed. And then he went on about how they all died in a ground collapse.'

'Ground collapse? I thought these guys won environmental awards,' said John.

'You tell me but he was on about it. I mean, people died, and he was talking as if he'd done really well. Well, Compo

Bonito, they called it. I'd never heard of it. He said that there were people trying to pin it on the excavations that had been done. And Corey had organised some works that had gone on. Well, he'd brought in the people who were doing it. When you hear him talk about it, you'd think he did it himself. But he organised the money to get out of it. He said he paid backhanders. He said that was how the world worked. I remember that line. He smacked me on the bottom when he said it. He was letting me know I was doing whatever he wanted. I hate him,' said Sylvia. 'But I love this wee guy. Look at him.'

John watched for a moment and for the first time, he felt truly comfortable watching someone else pick up little Ian. Even with Seoras, he was always watching him just to make sure he didn't drop him. It was irrational, yes, but the man had never had children. Neither had Sylvia, but he'd looked at the good that Ian was doing her, and John was quite an emotional man. It was a side of him that Hope loved, and he was fighting back a tear in his eye, watching this young woman holding what to her was a dream. He felt very privileged. He promised he would remind himself of that, the next time he had to change a nappy.

'Sylvia, we're heading down. Sylvia!'

Corey was shouting, but Sylvia didn't flinch. Instead, she yawned. 'Tell me if he moves back up,' she said to John, 'if you see him coming up the hill? I'll give you the wee one back, and I'll head off quickly. Otherwise, well, I'll pretend I haven't heard him.'

John stood up for a moment, carefully trying not to bring himself into the line of sight. But when he saw Corey with his back turned and walking down the slopes towards the main structure, he told Sylvia to rest at ease. He watched though as Corey had his arm around Emily, Alison's daughter, and he understood what Sylvia meant. It wasn't a fatherly hug. John saw the word 'predator' in his head and sat back down.

'He's heading off to the structure,' he said.

'Shall I give him back?' asked Sylvia. 'I've probably taken up too much of your time, telling you all my troubles.'

'No,' said John. 'You stay here and hold him. Tell me about yourself. I mean not what you do now. Tell me about yourself and where you came from. You're the most normal person outside of Hope I've found here. Take a break. Talk to me.'

Sylvia smiled and pulled little Ian closer to her. He gurgled again, a little hand coming up and tapping her on the chest. She looked down at him.

'One day,' she said, 'I'm going to have someone like you looking at him. I'm going to clear these debts, and I'm going to have a proper family.'

John smiled, looked out to the sea and listened as Sylvia told her life story to him. He couldn't do anything about it. At least he didn't think he could. But it was nice to hear her unload. Good to hear her talk about things that weren't false. He also realised that Sylvia knew a lot. Hope was out there trying to work out how to find out about these people, and here was John getting the dirt. Who'd have thought bringing a baby along would have given you access? He laughed inside as Sylvia continued.

Chapter 14

'Where have you been then?' asked Hope as John entered the pod.

'Been up on the hill talking to a prostitute,' said John.

Hope's eyes nearly popped out. 'You've been doing what?' she blurted out, half laughing.

'I was talking to Sylvia. She's the one with Corey Denman. Sweet girl. Sad story, though.'

'You were talking to her? How on earth did you get to talk to her?' said Hope.

'I took Ian with me. I tell you, he's terrific. You want to get behind what's going on? You need this little guy.'

Hope smiled and took him out of the baby carrier, holding him tight to her chest. 'And what did my two boys find out?' asked Hope. John related what Sylvia had told him about Compo Bonito. Hope stared at him, growing more intense in her look. 'Some sort of disaster then, excavations falling in,' said Hope. 'That's interesting, that's really interesting.'

'I just thought it was sad,' said John.

'That's the motive.'

'Motive? For what?' said John. 'What's happened?'

Hope stopped for a moment. John was right. Nothing had happened. As far as they knew, Ivor and Hannah and family were off in a hospital, Ivor recovering.

'You're talking like you're in the middle of a murder investigation,' said John. 'You've got one big problem.'

'Which is?' asked Hope.

'No one's dead,' said John. 'There might be some shenanigans going on at some point, but, you know, no one's dead. Everybody here looks very alive. A lot of idiots. A lot of tension. But nobody's dead. There's nothing for the detective to do.'

'Well, we haven't got a body but there are some indications of foul play,' said Hope, and she relayed what Laura had heard with the cleaners.

'They're speaking Brazilian Portuguese. That ties,' said Hope. 'They're talking in a way that could mean that Ivor didn't have long left. Now what does that mean?'

'Or it could have meant that Ozzie didn't have long left. They were going to get rid of him as a chef.'

'Ozzie didn't know about the rice either,' said Hope. 'You know what I wish. I wish Perry were here.'

'What?' said John.

'I wish Perry were here. Perry or Seoras, as they see things, you know. They see the connections.'

'Well, I for one am glad that they aren't here,' said John, 'because I was coming for a holiday with my partner and our little one.'

Hope smiled, but then she went back to a serious look again.

'I know that look. You need to relax, stay out of it. Just enjoy the next week and a bit.'

Hope walked over to the window, still carrying little Ian, and John came up behind her. He wrapped his arms around her waist.

'Be very careful,' he said. 'These people—they're not stable.'

'You just told me to keep out of it.'

'And I might as well tell Ian there not to poo in his nappy.'

Hope laughed. 'Am I that obvious? Am I really?'

'You really are to me. If you have to do it, be very careful. I mean that. You could upset these people easily. And they could go off half-cocked. Up in the shooting range, that scared me,' said John. 'I know you can handle yourself physically, but when there are weapons about, none of us can beat a weapon.'

'I know,' said Hope. 'I've also got this guy here to think about.'

'What is it you want to do?'

'I'm going to talk to Corey. You said he likes women, likes—'

'He's a predator.'

'Take the wee man,' said Hope, handing Ian over to John. She disappeared into the wardrobe. When she came back out, John gave a loud whistle.

'Seriously?' he said. 'Really? I'm not sure I'm comfortable with you going out dressed like that.'

Hope wore a tight crop top, along with tight leggings below it. John wasn't sure she was wearing anything else underneath it. But as he looked at her, she suddenly felt uncomfortable herself. And then she reached behind her and put her hair up in a ponytail. She looked over at him.

'This is work. I'm just playing the part.'

He walked over to her. 'I was worried about you, not what you would do,' said John. 'I have no worries on that side. Just be very careful. These guys take and don't think about what it is they're taking. He just uses Sylvia because he pays her. He won't necessarily look at you and think that he can't do the same.'

'Well, if he thinks that way and tries something, he'll soon get a knee between his jaffers,' said Hope. She kissed John. 'Thank you.'

'Get it out of your system. Go on,' said John.

Hope walked along the pontoon and into the main lounge, spying Corey getting himself a drink at the bar.

'Well, hello there. Now, that's what I call a proper housewife,' said Corey, staring at Hope.

'You got a drink there for me?' she said.

'Absolutely. What do you want?'

'Vodka,' said Hope. 'Just make it neat. In fact, bring the bottle. Let's go over there. It's quieter in that corner,' said Hope.

Corey walked over with her and plonked himself down on the sofa. On Hope's right hand was a large plant, which was about to get a large dose of vodka.

'Somebody told me you're a big shot.'

'Who said that?'

'Sylvia,' said Hope. 'Said you're a big shot, doing a lot of work down in Brazil. I fancy Brazil.'

'Brazil,' he said. 'Well, Brazil is something else. Do you know how they dress in Brazil? A bit like you. You'd look good down there on the beach. Done well after having a sprog too.'

Hope was ready to hit him for that one. But she didn't. Instead, she smiled. 'What do you do?' asked Hope.

'I make things happen, baby,' said Corey, to which Hope nearly burst out laughing. 'I'm the one in charge, the one who dominates. The one who makes people listen. See the rest of the people here? They couldn't do what they do without me. I'm a mover and shaker. I work for the US government down there.'

'What sort of things?'

'Find areas that have decent ores and minerals underneath. Extract them. Good for high-tech stuff. Down there, you can move on the population, get them out, get in, take what you want and then dump it all back.'

'Don't you get trouble with the locals?' asked Hope.

'The locals? Nah, even the police aren't an issue. They're not a problem. We had a job where the ground just collapsed.'

At this point, Federico and Stephen had entered and heard Corey talking loudly. They came over just as he was finishing his speech.

'Bonito Campo,' said Federico. 'That's why this man's in the team.'

'I'm not on the team. I'm leading the team,' said Corey.

'Like hell,' said Stephen, 'but you earned your money that time.'

'It earned us all a lot of money,' said Federico. 'If that had gone wrong . . .'

'Corey said there was some sort of collapse,' said Hope.

'Ground collapsed,' said Federico, 'number of the locals died and they tried to blame it on us. But you can't blame us, you can't place blame like that; money says where the blame is.'

'Why did you do something wrong?' asked Hope.

The three of them laughed. 'Mining's not an exact science,' said Corey suddenly. 'Mining is dangerous, risky, but it pays well, and it pays its way out of the difficult stuff.'

'I'll drink to that,' said Federico. He raised his glass, and Hope had to take a drink of her own, despite not wanting to.

'Anyway, I don't see what you're doing with that man,' said Corey. 'You look like the sort of filly that could keep a guy like me entertained.'

'You should be ashamed,' said Hope, punching him gently

on the arm. What she wanted to do was plant her fist in his face, but she would have broken cover.

'He let you off the leash for a while, has he?' said Stephen.

'Leave her alone,' said Frederico. 'That man is good. That man, he earned me money.'

Terence arrived suddenly and saw the three men huddled around Hope. He came over and listened to the conversation for a moment. And then he said, 'What is it you do?'

'I'm a housewife,' said Hope. 'I've said that before.'

'Bit too hot for a housewife. Good shape for a housewife too.'

'Isn't she?' said Corey. 'Doesn't she look good.'

'Well, I'm afraid, gentlemen, I have to see to a little one. Maybe we'll talk again.'

'Maybe indeed,' said Corey. 'I'd like that.' As Hope stood up to walk away, she heard Corey speaking behind her. 'God, look at that ass.'

Hope maintained her wiggle and walk until she'd left the lounge. As she strode along the pontoon, she thought she could hear someone behind her. She wondered who it was, then pretended that something had gone wrong with her shoe. She bent down to fix it and could hear the footsteps coming along behind her. They were trying to be furtive, but she could hear them, nonetheless. As she stood up, an arm went around her, pulling her to one side, and up against one of the pods. The hand went to her throat. Terence was looking straight into her eyes.

'Who the hell are you?' he said.

Hope drove her knee up into the man's stomach, and she thought he was going to be sick, she hit him so hard. His hand instantly let go, and she turned him around, pushing him up against the pod, and putting her hand on his throat.

'I said I'm a housewife, but I also know how to handle myself. I've done the training. For some reason, guys seem to like me. And sometimes I like to play on the edge, so I know what to do. Don't treat me like that. Next time I'll make it permanent.'

'Sorry,' said Terence suddenly, clearly worried. 'It's just, we've had reporters looking in. Reporters asking about Brazil, scared it's going to stir up a shitstorm. It should be dead and gone; it should be buried; it's done. I've had threatening letters, and you, well, you fitted the type.'

'There's only one type I fit,' said Hope, 'and that's me. I like to mess about with men, but I don't like to be messed about. So, you keep your hands to yourself, and we'll say no more. If I want to play the boys for a little bit of fun, I'll do it. Not easy when you have had little attention for a while,' she said, lying through her teeth. 'When my husband struggles, I'm just having some fun, okay? I'm no threat to you,' said Hope. 'So, hands off.'

'Okay,' said Terrence. 'I think we understand each other.'

'Good,' said Hope. She turned away, walked down to her pod and entered. When the door closed behind her and she saw Ian on the bed lying beside John, she held her pose for a moment. The pair of them were asleep. She wondered what she was doing, acting like she had.

Yes, she knew she was doing it to fit cover. She knew she was trying to tease out what was going on, but was it worth this? Was it worth putting them in jeopardy? Had she? What if Terence had been a bit more forward, put a gun in her back? John had said it. These people were unstable. She took off her shoes and came to lie beside John in the bed. He opened his eyes.

'Go well, did it?'

'It was hard,' she said.

'Did you find anything out?'

'The Brazil thing's serious,' she said. 'But I had four of them hovering around me. I don't know how that girl Sylvia can do it. They just look at you, talk at you like you're—'

John pulled her close. 'Just stay here for a minute. I'll look at you differently.'

'Good,' she said, and curled up into him.

Chapter 15

Hope was bothered. Something wasn't right, and she needed to check it out. Normally, she'd have gone to Ross, and Ross would have come back with all the newspaper reports, all the TV reports, lots of detail, everything. She realised what a right hand he was, and quite often, she didn't appreciate it. She would appreciate it now, though. Instead, she would have to find out second-hand, possibly even third hand.

The people who would know about the disaster, who really knew about it, were laughing about it last night. She could try to talk to Alison, but looking at the woman, she didn't think she could connect. That was the difference. When you came in and said, 'I'm DI McGrath', people were expected to answer your questions. They might have tried to evade giving the answer, but you had a platform to start from.

Alison had shown no interest in her, but she had a daughter, Emily. Maybe Hope could talk about little Ian with her, but the woman hadn't come over. Hope had found that when you introduced a baby into a room, there were those women who migrated to you, almost like a sisterhood. There were others who did not, uninterested in other people's children even if they were good mothers. Alison didn't seem bothered.

The men were easier, especially these types of men. With the figure she was blessed with, her height, her red hair, Hope could easily attract those men. Though she'd have to play such a horrid part to do it. She felt sick at times within herself. The only other person who might know, though, was Laura. She'd been friendly to Hope, and she'd almost seemed a little insecure, offloading some of her issues to Hope. Maybe she'd offload a little more.

Hope found Laura in the lounge and suggested that they go for a jacuzzi together. Laura readily jumped at the chance, for once again Paul seemed to be a little aloof. They joined up together some ten minutes later, closing the door of the private room and setting the bubbles going within the jacuzzi. Both women went down under the water, only their heads remaining above, and Hope thought it was divine. But she was here to work.

'I was talking to some of the other men here,' said Hope.

'I rarely get to talk to them,' said Laura suddenly. 'I'm sort of on the other side. Alison's the only one they really talk to. The rest of us, well, I don't know if you've seen the other ones with their wives. The men congregate together. Yes, they come together at a time with the wives, but the wives know their place. I'm worried sometimes that I'll end up like that. Stuck as just a wife there, and all you've got is the money. I don't want the money. I want Paul with me.'

Hope thought Laura was in the wrong company to think like that. But she didn't want to tell her that right now.

'The men were talking about Brazil.'

'It was a big thing for them,' said Laura. 'Really big. A lot of money was made from that. I know that, but I don't know how much. Not all the figures and details. Paul doesn't share that sort of thing with me. But when I was down, Corey was telling me all about how he'd made everything happen, and how there was money flowing here, there, and everywhere.'

'The men said that some of their work was quite dangerous. In one place, the ground had collapsed. Bonito Compo, they called it.'

'Yes. That's true,' said Laura. 'Paul's had some abusive letters about it. He was involved. They were all involved, in fact. I think that's true. Well, they were all down in Brazil working together. I don't know the contract details and that, but I remember going out at night with them all together, and at times, the men, and Alison of course, they would pop off for a discussion for a half hour, leave the rest of us to just talk. I found that difficult, because the others, they're . . . well, older than me.'

'What about Sylvia?'

'Sylvia wasn't there. Sylvia's for hire. Don't get me wrong,' said Laura, 'there's nothing with her. I get along with her. She's okay. The other women treat her with absolute disdain, but then I can get that. They, I think, see themselves as providing something for their husbands. She's just providing sex for Corey, isn't she? She's just there to be shown off. Paul shows me off sometimes, I think.'

'Yes, but you're not being paid to be shown off, are you?' said Hope. Inside, though, she thought it was such a toxic place. She felt like she should tell the girl just to run. 'They said people died in the incident, though,' said Hope.

'They did. And Paul had the letters of abuse. I remember watching him open them. He was bothered by it. Really bothered by it.'

'Well, did he not do anything to help?' asked Hope.

'He didn't know about it at the time. It was only after when it came to light. At first, as far as Paul knew, it was a natural disaster. And then he realised that, well, from what I can gather,' said Laura, 'and I'm no expert on this, some of the excavation work wasn't right. However, that was never proved in court. It's maybe why he's aloof at the moment. He's angry at being here with this lot.

'He made money out of it, yes, but he also wasn't happy with what Corey did. I mean, the trouble with the court case was that Paul wasn't involved with sorting it out. He didn't like paying their way out. You know, a lot of it was to do with the excavation work. Paul was taking the minerals that came out and feeding into his chain because of all the tech he works with. So, he kind of felt bad. He'd already put money down on this place. Part of the profit coming out of there was to go into this place. And look at it now. This will be a gold mine for him. He knows that. He said that to me. Once we have this initial stay and then it'll blow up. They'll make a fortune.'

'Is he okay with that then?' said Hope.

'He's kind of tied into the contract so he can't get out of it,' said Laura. 'That's what I think. However, he's not happy. He's really not happy about having come here and the rest of them being here.'

'He could leave, though,' said Hope. 'I'm not being funny. It's different for me. I won this. I can't really turn around halfway through and say, "Get me off."'

'Put more costs on them. They wouldn't want you to anyway,' said Laura. 'You're here to give something back. In fact, the only reason you're here was Paul said that we should get somebody and give something back to the people who make us what we are. He's very much like that. So, he did the raffle for charity, and you won. But you'll be expected to go back on the mainland and say to people how wonderful it is and all that. You don't get something for nothing, do you?'

'I guess not,' said Hope.

Laura sat up in the bubbles for a moment and then lay back again.

'I sometimes wonder about Paul. He seems mixed up in all of this, and I don't know if his heart's in it. Paul's quite the tech guy, and he also loved Brazil. He loved the people. He said that to me—said it was great down there. I think part of him liked the fact that I learnt Brazilian Portuguese and that I spent some time down there. He seems . . . I don't know. I'm finding it hard to connect with him at the moment. He seems a bit out of sorts.'

'Maybe it's being amongst all the rest of them. If he thinks something wrong went down,' said Hope, 'I could understand that he'd be annoyed.'

'It really is a crazy coincidence, isn't it?' said Laura. 'Their all being here for the first time, all together. I mean, to make it so that all the schedules work. That's the thing about them. They're usually all over the place, all CEOs with schedules. They're all, you know, being dragged here, there, and everywhere. And now we've got two weeks. At least we got two weeks together.'

As they were lying there, there was a brief knock on the door before it opened. Corey stood there, looking in. 'Hello, ladies,' he said. 'I might get my trunks. Are we needing trunks at all? I can't tell you're so far down in the water.'

Laura looked over, almost disgusted at the man, but Hope gave him a wink. 'Maybe next time,' she said. 'I'll have to go feed the little one.'

'Pity,' said Corey. Hope waited until he closed the door before she then got up and out of the jacuzzi.

'I'd better see to the little one. Just feels like it's feeding time. You get that when you've got a little one. You just seem to know.'

'Very good,' said Laura. 'I'm going to stay here. I'll get out if Corey comes back. He's a creep. But he seems to like you.'

'I think Corey likes anything with legs and boobs,' said Hope, laughing. 'I don't think it's difficult.'

'Yes,' said Laura, 'I think you're right. I'm just glad Paul's not the same.'

Hope grabbed her dressing gown and wrapped it around her. Inside, she wondered if Paul was the same, although it was interesting what Laura was saying. Again, she wished she had Perry here, or Macleod. They got people. They got the subtle signs. *Think, Hope, think. What's really going on here?*

Hope padded out into the lounge and got an appreciative glance again from Corey. Terence looked away when she walked past. When she made it out onto the pontoons, she was on her own. The funny thing about walking from the lounge to your pod was that you had to go outside. And now her body felt cool, almost cold, after having been in the warm jacuzzi.

As she sauntered down to her pod, she saw the one at the end had its door open. It was a pod that nobody used. Hope got to the door and looked inside. Checking back along the pontoon, and seeing nobody was there, she stepped inside. There were several tins of paint stacked up, brushes too. There was what looked like banners, but with no artwork on them. A cardboard box contained fixative tape and lots of string.

Hope wondered what it was because everything else around

here was classy. There was nothing roughshod. Nothing that was taped together, hung together. Everything had its own design. Everything was particularly well made. And here were a load of paint and brushes and a tarpaulin.

She was bemused. The door was open. Then she thought, who's about? This door has been closed the whole time. She thought she should get out, but then she heard footsteps on the pontoon. Quickly, she walked over to the window. This pod was on the end. You couldn't see any of the other pods from it, but it had a unique view. She stood there looking out as the footsteps got closer.

'Hello,' said Hamish, suddenly. Hope turned, and the man was standing there, smiling. 'What are you doing in here?' he said. 'I'm afraid this isn't set up. We've just stored a few extra bits and pieces in it, because we have got little room back in our own place. Normally, this would be a guest's quarters. So, I'm going to have to get it into shape for when the next lot comes. It shouldn't be too long after. I think they'll be booking up like anything, especially once you get back and people find out about it.'

'It's quite something from here, isn't it? The view,' said Hope. 'It's different to the rest.'

'Yes, it is,' said Hamish, standing beside her. 'Is there anything you wanted in here?'

'No, no,' said Hope. 'I was just walking down to mine and the door was open. And, well, nobody's been in this pod. I wondered if it was a special one. Something slightly different, but—'

'No,' said Hamish. 'It's the same as all the rest. Same wonderful one like all the rest. As I said, we just stored some extra bits of paint and that. There are a few stanchions and things we have to work on underneath just to finish off, which you can't see.'

'Oh, right,' said Hope. 'But yes, I came in and then I saw the view, and I thought, I need to see that.'

'Just been for a swim, have you?' asked Hamish.

'Just been in the jacuzzi with Laura. It's something else too. It's great just to have a relax.'

There was a sudden silence in the room, and she could feel that Hamish was waiting for her to leave.

'Anyway, you're clearly busy,' she said. 'I'll get out, okay?'

'Oh, I'm sorry to rush you. But you should see the seabirds today. That would be a good idea. They're quite something. The birds up on the cliff, late afternoon. Quite something to see. Why don't you come with us? In fact, I think everybody should go. Spread the word,' said Hamish.

Hope could feel him watching her as she left the pod. As she reached her own, she heard the door of the other pod slide closed. *What were they doing with paint? There was something here. Something's going on,* Hope thought.

Inside her own pod, she saw John with Ian. She gave a smile at them, but her mind was running. *Everyone in Brazil together. Everyone is suddenly here. Paul, a little shocked by it. Now we've got the other pod with paint and stuff in it. We've got a comment from our cleaners. Terrence worried about reporters. But like John said,* she thought, *no body. There's no body. This isn't a murder investigation. So, what is it? What's got my back up?*

She strolled over to the window of the pod, looking out. It dawned on her. She was doing what Macleod did. He used to do it in her office. Stand there and, look out the window. Now he did it in his own office, but complained bitterly about the view. Well, she didn't have any problems with the view. It was spectacular. She just couldn't put her finger on what was wrong.

Chapter 16

Hope stood before the window, musing. She'd been there for over an hour. Behind her, John picked up little Ian, who'd woken up.

'I think it's dinnertime for him.'

'Yes,' said Hope, but didn't turn round.

'That usually means you,' said John.

'Oh yes,' said Hope. She sat down on the bed, took Ian off John, and positioned him to let him feed. Once he was comfortable feeding, she continued to stare at the window from the bed.

'I'm not happy, John.'

'Really?' said John. 'After all this time, I just couldn't tell.'

She looked over at him. 'Seriously not happy. Something's up. There's something not right. My gut tells me something is wrong.'

'I realise that,' said John. 'But what are we going to do about it?'

'Do about it,' said Hope. 'You were the one telling me I should relax and take it easy. Just enjoy the holiday.'

'I'm the partner of Hope McGrath. Hope McGrath cannot relax when she thinks something's wrong. I married a detective, and something's ticking in that mind. There's no point in telling you to be quiet. There's no point in begging you to leave it alone, because you will want to know what it is. You will want to satisfy yourself that it's nothing. And the problem is that if there is something in that head, it's usually not nothing. So, what are we going to do about it?'

Hope looked down at Ian, attached to her breast, then up at John. 'John, we need to do this safely. We need to try not to provoke these people. You need to keep an eye on this one at all times. Nothing matters more than Ian.'

John came over to the bed, knelt on it, and kissed Hope's forehead. 'That's something you don't have to tell me,' he said. 'What's your plan?'

'Hamish said there was something to do with seabirds this afternoon. He was trying to get everyone to go.'

'I don't think that's a wise move,' said John.

'Why?' asked Hope.

'You're asking what's wrong. Something's up. And now Hamish is bringing everybody together. Think about it. When was the last time Hamish brought everybody together? It was on the first day. And then he said you're free to do whatever. Why is he bringing everyone together?'

'When did you become a detective?' said Hope.

'Just seems strange to me. Very strange.'

'I think I'll do a bit of poking around.'

'What sort of poking around?' asked John.

'The only place we haven't seen is the workers' quarters.'

'But you have seen it. You were taken through by Hamish.'

'Not everywhere. Only to a point. And I was there with Hamish.'

'And what does that mean?' asked John.

'He could have taken me to the places he wanted. He could have stopped me from seeing things. I think I saw most of the places, except for the workers' own living quarters.'

'What do I do then while you do that?' asked John.

'You stay here, in this pod. You don't go out.'

'Hamish wants everybody to meet up in the lounge at four, for these seabirds.'

'Well, I want to check things out. So, I'll try to do it before four. If something's up and he's bringing people together, that could be a time when he's looking to do something.'

'I'll stay put then,' said John. 'Ian and I will stay here. You do what you need to do.'

Hope waited until Ian had finished feeding, then handed him to John for winding. She dressed this time in what she thought of as her working clothes, jeans, her hiking boots, and a tight black t-shirt. She found a fleece and pulled it on over the top.

John looked at her, eyes full of worry, as he held Ian. Hope came over and hugged and kissed him.

'Be careful. Stay out of the way,' she said. She turned to look in the mirror. Her hair had been wet after coming out of the jacuzzi. She grabbed the brush and ran it through briefly before tying it up behind her in a ponytail.

'Working then,' he said.

'Working, yes.'

She saw him watch as she made her way across the room. A part of her felt awkward at leaving. She wanted to stay and protect them. But she didn't know there was an actual threat yet. Something was just up, and she needed to see what it was and what to do about it.

'I trust you,' said John before she opened the door. 'I trust you. If you think something's up, something's up. Go find out.'

She gave a grin back and opened the door, stepping out onto the pontoon. As she went towards the main lounge, everywhere felt quiet. Maybe some of the guests were up at the range for she could hear gunshots. There was only Ollie faffing around, moving various bits of food into the kitchen area of the lounge. Hope came up behind him.

'Excuse me,' she said, clocking that Ollie had a pass. 'Can you tell me something?' Ollie sort of half grunted, and Hope pointed towards some of the fruit. 'What type of fruit is that? I've never seen it before.'

Her right hand, however, reached over, taking the pass that was clipped on the side of Ollie's belt from him. She slipped it into her pocket as the man tried to mutter some words in English but clearly he was struggling to describe what the fruit was.

'Never mind,' said Hope.

She turned away and sat down in the chair momentarily. Ollie disappeared back into the workers' quarters, then walked through the lounge towards the pontoon leading to the pods. Hamish appeared on the other side of the door. They walked down the pontoon, and Hope reckoned they must have been heading to the unused pod. She thought about following them, but instead, she took the device that she'd been given at the start for safety, popping it into the plant pot in the lounge. Then she made for the workers' quarters.

Hope strode through, to where she'd been previously, but things were different this time. The area was more of a mess, with items left here and there. She walked past a cardboard box. It appeared to have some food in it. But why leave it here? Everything on the retreat was usually so orderly.

It wasn't all the same food. It was an array of foods, like something you would take for a packed lunch. Hope walked on, listening intently.

She got to the workers' quarters and used Ollie's card against the door access control, which opened the door. She'd never been in here before, and the corridor led to six other doors. Hope tapped on one of the access pads, but the door didn't move. She tapped on more and they didn't move either. Not until she got to the last one.

The door slid back, and walking in, Hope gasped. There was a large Brazilian flag on the wall, and a picture of a woman and some children. There were also other pictures of what looked like a disaster. Ground that had caved in.

Ollie was Brazilian, wasn't he? Did he come from the area? Did he know of it? Was this the disaster they'd been talking about? The ones they'd all laughed over?

Hope looked down and saw a bag that was packed. There were no clothes put aside. *Was Ollie ready to go?* Hope searched the drawers here and there, wondering if there might be any weapons. *But why packed? What was the plan here?*

She froze as she heard someone in the corridor outside. Ollie's door had slid closed not long after she'd entered the room, and Hope pulled herself down tight, hiding in a small wardrobe space.

Someone spoke what Hope thought was Brazilian and banged on the door. Footsteps followed that faded quickly as if someone was walking away. Somebody was looking for Ollie but clearly didn't know where he was. She breathed out in relief.

The fleece she had on was warm. But it was a wise precaution because she didn't know where she would have to go. But inside here, holding her breath, she could feel the sweat running down her cheeks, under her armpits. Everywhere was warm, and she was tense. When she'd gone to find if something was wrong here she hadn't expected this.

She opened the door of Ollie's quarters and stepped back into the corridor. There was nowhere else in this little section to go, for all the other doors were locked. It made sense for the access cards to only work on their own quarters, but maybe Ollie had access to everywhere else. Hope left the corridor back to the main section she'd come from and crept down towards the radio room. Everything looked dead. Panels unlit. There was no power at the unit. Slowly, she crept back out.

As she walked down the corridor, she thought she could smell something. Something off. No, it wasn't. Her detective senses were coming to the fore. That wasn't something off. That was—please no—she knew the smell. It was the smell of death. The smell you got when you went to see a deceased body that had been left there for a while.

Everything within Hope went on red alert. She crept along the corridor, sliding towards the medical room she'd been in previously. Using Ollie's credentials, she tapped the keycard at the door, and it slid open. Hope almost coughed, but, putting a hand over her nose, she stepped inside, allowing the door to close behind her.

The medical room didn't look that different. There were items here, there, and everywhere, but the smell was so strong. She looked around the room and saw a tall and deep cupboard. She hadn't seen inside it before and was unsure of what was there as it had remained unopened when she'd been taken on the tour. This time she walked over slowly, carefully, and began to open the door.

At first, the door was opening slowly, but then she heard something move and the door raced violently at her. Something was tumbling out, and Hope stepped back quickly, stumbling backwards.

She'd seen many horrific things in her life. Once she'd even come across a decapitated head but this was a sight she would never forget. Ivor tumbled out first, lifeless, dead and thumping hard on the floor. On top of him fell Hannah, his wife, and then two kids.

Hope went down to her knees, desperate to breathe in air, but couldn't use her nose because of the smell, and tried to gulp in through her mouth. *Steady,* she said to herself, *steady. You don't want to cause a fuss; you don't want anyone to know you're here.*

Slowly, she made her way over to the bodies that had tumbled out onto the floor. She took a quick check around Ivor but could see nothing that was unusual. However, Hannah's throat had been slit, and those of the children as well.

The children. Hope could feel her eyes beginning to water. She was hit by the anger of a mother, the rage building inside of her. She clenched her fist, fighting to hold it down. Of course, it was wrong. Her mind swam with little Ian. She would rip apart whoever did this to those poor kids. And then she tried to tell herself to pull it together. *She was a detective. There'd been murders. Who was at further risk? What was next? Think!* she told herself. *Think!*

Maybe Ivor had indeed had a reaction; maybe Ollie had made the mistake. Ollie had given him milk. He'd reacted, but he was going to be flown away. But somebody didn't want him to fly away. Somebody wanted him here. So much so that they let him die and then killed his wife and kids. Simply. Very simply. That's why there was no helicopter. That's why she couldn't hear it. Everybody had to be kept here.

What was this place? This was a place where you were alone. This was a place that nobody else would see. Nowhere else could reach here. If you harmed people here, you could be gone before word would reach anyone. No one would know. For ages. Days.

Hope could feel the hairs on her neck rise. In truth, she shivered a little. She thought of John. Of Ian. *Four o'clock. It was four o'clock now. This was four o'clock. Hamish was gathering people. What for? Just what exactly for?*

Chapter 17

Ian was somewhat agitated, so John put him inside the baby carrier and paced up and down the pod. He stared out of the large window, but it didn't seem to provide him much comfort. He didn't like Hope being away like this. As much as he'd thought that she was overreacting—her detective instincts needing a run out—John was becoming worried that she actually was right in this case.

He hadn't been involved in much of Hope's work, save for the time when she was attacked at Inverness Hospital. It wasn't John's world, and it certainly shouldn't be wee Ian's world. It was coming to four o'clock, and he could hear everyone else on the move on the pontoons. Hamish wanted them all gathered together in the lounge, a walk to see the birds.

It was wrong. Hamish had said he would leave everybody alone. He wasn't organising anything. And then, all of a sudden, he had everyone going off to see the birds. John hoped it was something Hamish had noticed. But Hope had been out to see the birds before. It wasn't something that John thought was essential, and also at one particular time? Why at four in the afternoon?

It was getting dark. In fact, it was getting dark quickly. What would you see? How would you see? John continued to pace and then noticed Ian was purring. He sometimes wondered if that was the boy's favourite activity. Just to curl up either on his mum or dad's chest and go to sleep.

The door of the pod rang. Ian waited for a moment until it rang again. There would be someone looking for them to come up to the main lounge. He went to the door and opened it.

'Time to go look at the birds,' said Hamish. 'Everyone else is assembled. We're just waiting for the two of you. Sorry, you three,' he said. And then he stopped for a moment. 'Where is your partner?'

'Oh, Hope went off earlier. I'm just looking after the wee man. I don't think we'll come. He's a bit agitated. You don't want a crying baby in the middle of looking at the birds.'

'But it's something quite special,' said Hamish. 'You need to come.'

'But how are we going to see them?' asked John. 'I mean, wouldn't it be better just to get a night's sleep and see them in the morning?'

'It's special at this time of day,' said Hamish. 'You really must come and see them. We must find Hope and bring her too. What was she off to do?'

'She went for a wander. Looking after this wee man, it tires you out, so she didn't say where she was going. She just went. You learn, Hamish, that in these early days you have to give each other a bit of space when you can. A bit of time to recharge the batteries. She could be anywhere.'

John saw Hamish's eyes narrow. 'Well, she really needs to come, as do you. Come along.'

'I've got a baby asleep,' said John. 'I don't want Ian disturbed.'

'I appreciate that,' said Hamish, 'but I really must insist. Everyone is coming up to the lounge. When you get there, you'll find out it'll be worth it. Trust me. We'll make sure the wee man doesn't wake up.'

'How are you going to manage that? I'm managing that at the moment. I am walking slowly up and down in front of this window barely keeping him settled,' said John.

'You can walk up and down in the lounge. Come,' said Hamish. 'If we don't go now, we're going to miss it. It's a very special thing.'

'What do they do exactly, these birds?' said John.

'It's hard to explain. You need to see it,' said Hamish. 'Please come.' His hand was now on John's shoulder.

'I don't know,' said John.

'No, you need to come, come.' Hamish was now almost dragging John towards the door.

'I'll just get my coat then,' said John.

'Your coat?' queried Hamish.

'If we're going outside to see the birds, I'll need my coat on. Wrap up Ian, keep him warm.'

'Good idea,' said Hamish. 'Yes, yes.'

John walked into the open wardrobe and put on a coat, wrapping it around him. He also found some gloves and stuffed them in the pockets. There was a hat there too. When Hamish couldn't see him inside the wardrobe, he stuck in a coat of Ian's and a few blankets. He wasn't happy with what was going on, not one bit.

'Are you ready? Come on, come on, we need to go quickly.'

Hamish almost whisked him out of the door when John came back out of the wardrobe, practically pushing him along the pontoon. As John arrived at the lounge, he saw everyone was there, except Hope. The staff were all gathered, as well as all the guests. Some of them seemed a little flustered.

'What exactly is this that happens?' asked Terence.

'Shut up and let the man deal with it,' said Paul, suddenly. 'He's going to show us something. Hamish says it's wonderful. He's not going to drag us all out like this unless he thinks it's that good, is he?'

'Has anyone found Miss McGrath?' asked Hamish. And then when he saw faces of incomprehension, he said, 'Hope, the mother of the young child.'

'I haven't seen her,' said Laura.

'Then where is she?' cried Terence suddenly.

'She went off for a walk while I looked after the little one,' said John.

'Oh, we must find her. She can't miss this,' said Hamish.

'And why can't she?' said Alison. 'If she's not good enough to get her backside here for it, well then she can miss it.'

'She's our guest here,' said Hamish. 'We really can't afford for people to be missing it.'

'Well, I think you're wrong,' said Alison Mathers. 'I'll give the woman two minutes. Anyway, you stated here at four o'clock. You said we'd miss it. It's going to start soon, whatever it is, isn't it?'

'We have a little bit of time,' said Hamish, but he was clearly flustered.

John manoeuvred himself out of the central congregation of the group, over towards the door that led out to Boreray. He wondered where Hope was, and he watched as Hamish disappeared quickly off to a laptop.

'We'll find her,' he said. 'We'll find her in no time.'

'Yes, where is she? We've all got one of those things, haven't we? We've all got one of those things. You should be able to find where she is.'

John felt down his left side and towards the pocket where he kept his detection device. They'd said it was there for safety. There in case you fell in, or you became trapped somewhere in Boreray. They'd know where you were. He reached into his pocket and took it out. He hoped, in fact he prayed, that Hope had been as sensible. John carefully placed his inside a flowerpot beside where he was standing.

Hamish came back from the computer. His face looked like thunder.

'Well?' said Terence. 'Where is she?'

'It says she's here in this room,' said Hamish. Cupboards were opened, and they tore around the place in what seemed a rather frantic effort.

'Well, those devices aren't much good, are they? What did we pay for them?' shouted Alison Matthews. 'Come on, we need to go. Lead us on.'

'No, we need to wait for her. We need to have her here,' insisted Hamish.

'The man's right,' said Paul. 'We don't want to leave her behind. She's our guest. We made her feel welcome here. We need to make sure she's not left out.'

'Who cares?' blurted Frederico. 'She can't be bothered to be here. Then we need to go. Yes?'

'Well, that's it,' said Alison Matthews. 'I'm going.' She marched over towards the door leading to the pontoon to the pods. But the door wouldn't open. 'What's going on with this?'

'I'm afraid that I have something to tell you,' said Hamish. He was now standing with a gun produced from his pocket.

The rest of the staff suddenly produced weapons too. 'If you'll all kindly take a seat,' said Hamish.

'What are you doing?' said Alison Mathers. 'We employ you, man. What are you doing?'

Hamish fired a shot straight into Alison Mathers' foot. She screamed, tumbling to the ground. Her daughter bent down quickly, but Hamish grabbed her by the shoulder and threw her into a chair.

'Sit down, everyone! Everyone, sit down! And bloody well shut up!' Terence was late to sit down, and Hamish cracked him across the top of the head with the gun. Terence collapsed.

'Do you want money? Is it money you want?'

'Money,' spat Hamish, looking at Corey, who had made the comment. 'You only understand money. All of you bastards killed them. You killed our people. Now we will kill you. The world will see what you are, all of you.'

'What on earth?' shouted Paul. 'What do you mean?'

Hamish slapped him across the face. 'Sit there and shut up, or she'll be next.' Hamish put his gun to Laura's forehead.

The woman shook, turning white. 'No, no, no, please, please, no.'

'Okay,' said Paul, 'everyone, just sit, okay? Just sit for a minute.'

Alison Mathers was still screaming. Ollie walked over holding a large shotgun, and he drove the barrel into the side of her head, knocking her out cold. He said something in another language and then resumed his former position. Hamish turned to the rest of the staff, said something in a different language, and they went into the cupboards around the lounge. They emerged from their rifling with handcuffs, and one by one, handcuffed all the guests.

'You're going to feel what it was like. You're going to understand what you did. And so will the world. Everyone will. People meant nothing to you. Nothing,' cried Hamish.

He spat in Paul's face . The bubbles of the globular mass descended Paul's cheek as he could not wipe it clear, his hands now handcuffed. Hamish was stalking every one of them.

'Tell me. Tell me where she is. Anyone. Where is she?'

It was then that Geordie, one of the cleaning staff who had been handcuffing the guests, held up two handcuffs to Hamish.

'Two,' he said, scanning around him. There was no sign of John with little Ian in his baby carrier.

Scene break, scene break, scene break.

John thanked God he'd seen it coming. The desperation to get Hope into that room, everyone gathered together. What she had said about the disaster, what these people allegedly had done. John thought it was almost movie-like, but something had felt wrong. Hamish, so desperate to push him in, so desperate to get Hope back, to see some birds, was ridiculous.

So John had decided not to take the risk. The door had barely closed quietly when he'd seen Alison walk over to the door to the pods, and it had been locked. He'd been lucky. Hamish must have activated the locks when Alison walked over. At that point, John hadn't looked back. He'd crept along the path towards Boreray.

But where was Hope? Where was his beloved partner? He wondered whether he could warn her. But his job was not to solve this. His job would be to keep the wee man safe. That's what she would want. Besides, he was neither a skilled fighter nor a cunning detective. But where should he go?

It was dark outside now, although the pontoon he was currently walking along was lit. He needed to get off this; he knew it. The lights out of the harbour, or rather the mass of pontoons that served as one, were on as well. Boreray itself was in darkness, with only the lights of the shooting range and that of the viewpoint, and the lights of the paths leading up to them.

He could feel the wind beginning to whip up. There might be rain. Getting the coat had been a stroke of genius. Why had he done it? He had a feeling he was going to run, feeling he had to do something. They weren't going out to see the birds, he'd known that. He'd taken the blankets for little Ian, too.

As he walked away, the sound of the gunshot still rang in his ears. He knew he had to go quickly. Alison Mathers had fallen to the floor. He wasn't sure what Hamish had done. Had he killed her? Had he just injured her? He was also thankful he'd dropped his indicator. The beacon, they were all meant to wear, so they would know where they were. Hope had obviously done the same with hers.

John gritted his teeth and ran on. And then he thought, *I can't just run. If I hide somewhere, it'll be obvious. I need to give them something, other places to chase. After all, how do I get off here? Where do I go?*

He looked out at the sea and the water. He could send a boat out. In fact, he could go out in the rowboat. But he'd have no shelter. He would get soaked when the rain came. Cold combined with the wind was a recipe for death. He needed shelter. He had a little baby inside his coat, after all. No, he needed to stay either within the structure or within any of the other structures around the island. But he also needed to keep them off his trail until he found Hope, or until he knew what he was going to do.

Chapter 18

Hope was making her way back to the lounge, ready to pop back into the four o'clock meeting and try to assess the situation. But before she could, she heard the gunshot. There was a woman's scream, utter commotion, and it was through the door ahead. She could run through. She could check, run in and take charge of the scene, tackle whoever had the gun. But that would be crazy. After all, she would be so exposed, and she wasn't armed.

The commotion inside continued, and Hope returned to the medical room, where four bodies were now lying on the ground. She looked around for the scalpels, but they were gone. Had they taken anything dangerous, any item that could be a weapon?

Hope understood what had been happening that afternoon, Ollie running back and forward, Hamish going to the spare pod. They had been prepping for this all afternoon. But they had guns, so she would need to maintain her distance.

Hope crept back along the corridor, to the edge of the lounge, because she needed to see if John was there, and her little Ian. As she came closer, she heard the door about to open and she ducked back out of the way, running back into the medical room. A man raced past her, and Hope opened the door. She saw him disappear outside. She made her way back up to the lounge door, which was now lying open. Keeping herself out of sight, she listened and could hear Hamish inside the lounge.

'We will find them. We'll find them all. It won't be a problem. You two, go out that way. Anyway, check the harbour. Then we check the island. We look for the redhead as well. You shoot on sight. Remember, they're expendable. We can just dump their bodies. We need the rest of this lot.'

Hope could see the two cleaning staff, Ella and Geordie, making their way to the door that led out to the harbour. They had guns in their hands. Her heart skipped a beat. That's where John and Ian must be. She wondered how John got out. *Had he realised? Had he thought? Did he have his beacon on him?* Maybe he didn't. Maybe he had dumped it because they didn't know where he was. And they didn't know where she was. This was an advantage, clearly.

'You all know why you're here, I take it. Compo Bonito. You'll pay for your actions in Compo Bonito. You didn't even have the decency to pay compensation. Didn't have the decency to say we got it wrong. Instead, you actually ended up costing the people that brought the case money.'

'If you want money, you can have money,' said Stephen Winner. Hamish disappeared out of sight, but Hope thought she heard him hit Stephen with the gun butt. The man groaned.

'Money. All you can see is money. That's it, isn't it?'

Where had John gone? Or had he gone? Surely, they'd have checked the pod. Or maybe because she'd gone out, they thought he was out too. She'd have to get to the pod quickly. She couldn't walk through the lounge, anyway. Hamish was there.

Hope got to the door and glanced through. She clocked three staff. Well, two had run out the door. Ollie, she reckoned, was the one who had gone down this corridor. So, there were just the fitness instructors and Hamish in the room. Still, it was too many to take on at once, especially when they were all armed.

'The world will know about you, will find out what you did to those people. The obscenity, the money you made down there. You built this place for yourselves. You didn't give the money back. Not you, the filth of society. You wrecked the lives of those people. Destroyed their place. You wrecked everything around them. And then you had the gall to build this so you could all, what, lavish it up? To make more money? You disgust me. You all disgust me. But you'll pay for it.'

Hope realised she was standing in an awkward place now, just outside the door Ollie had exited through. She couldn't go into the room because there were three people with guns. Therefore, the obvious thing to do if she wanted to find John was to go out the rear where the helipad was, and go by water.

Hope wasn't worried about the water outside. The wind was picking up, and it was choppy, but she could swim. And she'd been underneath the structure. She'd seen it. You could come up underneath and still breathe. It would be dark and it would be awkward, but she could do it. She could go over and check the pod, and see if John was hiding inside.

Hope made her way back along the corridor, ignoring Hamish's continuing rant within the lounge. She got to the door that led outside to the steps up to the roof and the helicopter landing pad. Waiting for a moment, she couldn't hear anything. Carefully, she pressed the button for the door. It opened.

Hope stepped outside and let it close. On the wind, she heard someone stamping about up at the helicopter landing pad. Without hesitation, Hope dropped into the water from the pontoon she was standing on. She went under the water and then swam back in underneath the structure.

She was almost blind swimming but touched a steel pipe and followed it upwards until she cleared the water. There was maybe about a foot or two between the top of the water and the structure, and Hope took a deep breath. She put her hand out to find more of the structure. Touching another pipe, she allowed herself to drift on.

The water was freezing. She could feel the cold everywhere, numbing her. She'd go on for she had to. Finding another pole and then another cross piece, she kept her hands up to touch the structure above her. If she kept her hands on it, she couldn't lose where she was.

Keep yourself going forward and get to the other side, she thought. The pods were slightly separate from the main structure, and she might have to swim for them. They had a pontoon connecting them to the structure, but it was more open, more space with just water. That's why it allowed such a good view. She would also have to move quick. After all, the water was icy. She couldn't stay in it for that long.

Focusing on the task at hand and trying to push all thoughts of what had happened to John and wee Ian, Hope clambered across the bottom of the structure. Her body was in the water, but her hands worked the structure above her. She got to a point where she recognised the pontoon in front of her. It was the one leading to the pods.

No one seemed to be searching this way. Maybe John had been clever. Maybe he'd been able to hide within the pod. Had he gone for another pod? The one with the paint tins in it? How would he get in?

Reaching the pontoon, Hope clambered up onto it but stayed flat. The lights of the lounge could be seen, and the pontoon was lit as well. She crawled along until she reached her own pod and then stood up, taking the card that would activate the door and pressing it to the scanner. Hope stepped inside. At least in here it was warm.

She shook off the water, looked around and saw a room which, while not undisturbed, showed no signs of struggle. She raced into the extensive wardrobe. No sign of John or Ian. Hope checked the bathroom, checked under the bed, checked everywhere. She began feeling around the floor, wondering if there was some secret panel they might have crawled past into the works underneath. It was then that her hands came across something.

There was a piece of flooring that was sitting up ever so slightly. There were two screws on one side of it, but two were missing at the other side. She put her hand down and grabbed the panel. It wouldn't give way. On her knees, she used two hands and yanked at it. The panel snapped.

Hope looked inside. It was dark. There were pipes. Clearly, it wasn't somewhere that anyone could enter. She was about to leave it alone when she thought she saw something. Putting her hand in, she pulled out a vanilla envelope. She opened it and took out what seemed like plans. There were circles around certain bits. And then, at the end, was a handwritten note.

The boss was involved. Wild about Compo Bonito. All he ever talks about is Compo Bonito. They will pay for Compo Bonito.

Hope shivered. This had been planned. Planned.

A thought struck her. She'd activated the door. At some point, somebody could notice. That was the way of these electronic things. All systems had logins, had records of when systems had been activated—and she had activated the door of the pod. Therefore, they would know she was in here.

Would they wait for her to come out? She wouldn't go that way. Hope decided she would need to swim. It would give her the best opportunity to go and find John and Ian and maybe some way of protecting them and her.

She ran into the wardrobe, picked up a small bag, and began stuffing jumpers, t-shirts, and trousers inside. Socks too. She took off her shoes. They were soaking. Grabbing a fresh pair, she put them in the bag. Hope stripped down to her bra and knickers, leaving the wet clothes on the floor of the pod. She put the manila envelope inside the bag too.

Hope could hear them coming now. The pontoon had noisy feet on it. She pressed a button, opening the window at the front. When it was just wide enough, she stopped it, and clambered out. From the outside, she pressed another button, closing the window.

It was freezing, but she sank into the water, keeping the bag just above it on her head. With one hand, she swam along the edge of the pods, close enough so that anybody looking out the windows would struggle to see her. She swam around towards the harbour, and it took her several minutes. When she arrived, she saw people searching. So, she cut by and went underneath the structure again. It was difficult to keep the bag up, but she knew she had to. Her skin was frozen, but she kept kicking, kept her arms moving, telling herself she'd be out soon. She'd have to get dry and change quickly somewhere. As she emerged from the other side of the structure, she thought to herself; *I need a plan. What do I do?*

She was stuck on her own, with no weapons. The only way to communicate with the land was to get to the radio. It had been shut down, though, judging by what she had seen. The other way to get attention was to fire off a distress message, or set off an EPIRB—a device they activated when a boat went underwater. Hope needed to alert the authorities that there was a distress situation, and then she'd have to stay alive.

She'd have to keep clear of the guns, she'd have to keep clear of those hunting for her, and she'd have to find Ian and John with him. She needed to keep them safe, needed to keep them from harm. Yes, the detective in her said there were other people to watch out for, other people to save, but they were her first call, they were her first priority. They were hers!

Having stayed in the water for five minutes, and hearing no one, Hope clambered out. She shook herself down, and then changed into the clothing that was in the bag. She kept the envelope in the bag, and slung it over her shoulder. The best way to go was to get onto the island of Boreray, because clearly the structure itself wasn't a safe place to be. That's where they were operating from.

If she could get to the range, the lookout point, or somewhere up there, it would be a place to defend. Somewhere to hide out, and with shelter, because there was a storm coming in. The wind told her that. The breeze was rising; the sense of foreboding, probably from an air pressure change, said storm.

She went to go, and then something clicked in her mind. The information she'd found under the floor in the manila envelope said that the boss had gone crazy. But the boss who had built this—there wasn't just one. There were lots of bosses. But which boss did the writer mean? Who was the one who had given the instruction to make the changes that were outlined within the envelope? They were going to kill them in some fashion. That's what seemed to be indicated.

She would need time to sit and study what all the circles were about. But somebody here must have known about Hamish. This structure was built, commissioned by those who had committed the crimes down in Brazil. Somebody felt bad enough to do something about it. Somebody was angry enough. Or was somebody else taking out all the competition and using this to justify it? She'd have to figure it out. But the first priority was safety. Safety for her, but more importantly, safety for little Ian and John.

Chapter 19

John needed to think straight. It was hard. His heart was beating fast. He'd heard the gunshot. He had little Ian strapped to his chest. Fortunately, the wee one hadn't woken up and begun shouting. It wouldn't have surprised Ian, especially with the sound of gunfire. But he needed a plan. He needed to think.

They would come after him. After all, at some point they'd notice he wasn't there. He'd ditched the tracker, which gave him some confidence that he had the foresight to realise what was happening. But now he needed to go.

Yes, there were boats on the jetty. There were the jet skis, but they didn't have enough fuel to get anywhere else. Well, they could get over to Hirta, couldn't they? He didn't know how to ride a jet ski, let alone how to start one. They needed keys too. Would the keys even be there?

He made his way along the pontoon, but there were no keys in the ignition. There were the kayaks and rowing boats, though. John untied one of the rowing boats. He didn't want to be out there in that water, not with little Ian. It would be freezing when a storm blew in. So, he pushed the boat out and watched as the current took it, moving the vessel away from the structure.

He turned, ran back down the pontoon, and was about to walk away when he heard the noise of a door opening behind. Quickly, he hid behind a small shed on the pontoon. Geordie had come out, brandishing a gun in his hand. Beside him was Ella. She turned off to search another part of the structure, but Geordie went to the pontoon.

He stood looking, and John noticed he was counting. The hair on John's neck went up. This had to work; otherwise, the man would start coming towards the other shed on the pontoon. If he did, John might have to jump him. How did you jump someone with a baby strapped to you?

John heard a very faint murmur from his chest. He looked down and saw that Ian's eyes were beginning to open. He wrapped his arms around him trying to make the child feel warmer, to go back to sleep. John looked up.

Geordie was now untying one of the other boats. He took the oars, sat back, and rowed off. John looked for the other boat in the dark, but he couldn't see it. Geordie had a flashlight in his boat, but John couldn't wait to find out if the man saw the boat or not. As quietly as he could, and crouching as low as he could with a baby strapped to him, he hastened off the pontoon, down a connecting pathway and onto the island of Boreray.

The paths were lit, and John thought walking along them would be akin to suicide. They would see him from below. So, he tore off straight onto the grass. It was harder to walk here, but that didn't matter. He needed to get up and away. *The range,* he thought. *The range would be a good place. There were guns there.*

Maybe that would be enough to defend himself. He was no

shot, but he thought he could remember how Corey had loaded his shotgun. He certainly remembered where the ammunition was, and where the shotguns were.

Slowly, he crawled up the steep hill of Boreray towards the shooting range. It had a light on the outside, and the path up to it was lit. Otherwise, it was darkness all around. On his right-hand side he saw the other viewpoint with a small light on the outside, too.

He made his way slowly, clambering with the weight of Ian not helping. John reckoned he should kill the power when he got there. Would he be able to find the light switch? The trouble with that was it signalled that he was there. If they looked up and saw the lights gone, they would know he was there. Maybe he'd have to leave the lights on; it was a game of hide and seek that he truly didn't know how to play.

He prayed Hope was there. She knew how to handle these things. Hope didn't sit and wonder if she should do something. She just got on with it, the confidence bred into her from her time in the police force. But she was also six feet tall.

He stopped for a moment, seeing her before him. He remembered the first time he had seen her. It was in Inverness. She was walking around the town, and he just stopped and stared. Six feet tall, bigger than him, hair that flowed out and down her back. Her leather jacket had been open. The jeans were not tight but fitted her so neatly. She'd blown him away.

He had thought nothing of it; after all, someone like her was out of his league. Then she'd popped in that time she was hiring a car. Something had gone wrong with hers, and she needed to hire a car. John had been in the back room, and Lynn had been dealing with Hope. John, realising she was there through the office window, and it was that redhead, the one he'd seen in town, got into gear.

He told Jane that he would assist the customer to her car. But he couldn't quite remember how it had happened. He just started talking, and to his surprise, she clearly was interested. It had taken a few more dates and all the rest of it but truly that time they had just connected over being told the conditions and the status of a hire car.

John grinned, looking down at the wonder they had produced together, and gritted his teeth. It would not end here. John pushed on and felt the rain fall. Pulling his hood up, he was glad he had his coat on. John was struggling to see, but surely there was no one up here. Everyone had gone into the lounge except Hope. Unless they had other people who had arrived whom he hadn't seen.

John stopped himself. He was getting paranoid and just needed to get on with what he was doing. The die was cast, and he needed to stay alert. *Time to find a shotgun.*

'Dad's going to look after you, little Ian,' he said. 'Dad'll look after you while your mum kicks arse.' A shiver ran down his spine, despite his brave talk. He was so fearful—he couldn't lose her; he couldn't lose Hope.

John arrived at the edge of the shooting range, staying out of the light. If he went round to the front and came in that way, no one would see him. If he went to the doors at the rear, which was the normal entrance, of course they would. *The doors would probably be locked. No, they wouldn't,* he thought. *Why would they be locked? They were here for the guests, at any time, night and day. Although shooting at this time of night would be a little unsociable. Not that any of these moneymakers would care.*

John edged his way around to the front of the range. The

problem there was that it dropped away sharply, for it was perched on the edge of a cliff. He held tight to anything he could at the front of the range. The drop behind him was a mere couple of feet away, but it was a couple of hundred feet down, with the wind blowing and a baby to carry. It wouldn't be easy.

He leant in and slowly sidestepped his way around to the front of the range. He could see in the far corner the small hide from which the clay pigeons were fired. They whipped across sharply, and there was a zone painted you shouldn't stand in, lest you got hit by them. Why you would stand out here when they were being fired, John didn't know. Shooters would stand with a shotgun on the other side of you, firing through you to hit them. He made his way inside the range and looked over at the gun cupboards. They were lying open, and they were empty.

Of course they wouldn't be so stupid, would they? Why would they be so stupid as to leave guns here?

He looked in the ammunition cabinet and found none there either. *Then again, why would it be important? The ammunition would be rubbish without the guns.* He stopped for a moment, with an icy shiver running through his body again. *What was he to do? What do we do?*

'Your mum would know,' he said aloud to little Ian. The child had his eyes open now but wasn't saying much. John hoped that being wrapped up close to Dad was keeping him quiet. Keep the little guy alive; that was his job. But what else should he be doing?

John looked around and could see the fridge stacked with beer. There were all the whiskey bottles and other types of liquor. But there were also bottles of water. John searched the range, looking for a bag. He found one. It was a small laundry-type bag holding Hi-Viz vests. There were ear defenders, too. He tipped them out and tried slinging the bag over his shoulder. It would work.

He took bottles of water and put them in the bag. Then he looked around. Chocolate bars. Crisps. He took them too. They would keep him going, for he didn't know how long he would have to wait out here. Even if they got off the island and the structure, they'd need to survive. Food was important.

He looked down at Ian. There was only one person who could give him food. And John hoped he wouldn't be looking for it too soon. He stood in the middle of the range, listening to the driving rain outside. He realised he had a problem.

The range had its back to the structure, and you couldn't see out of it. You could see forward, to where you would shoot, but you had to step back outside of the range to see anyone approaching up the hill. The hill was steep. The path was lit. If you were outside, you could see, but John couldn't stand outside all night. The rain was driving hard, and he'd be soaked. His best chance would be to keep on the move. Take up a position to see if anyone was coming and then move in the dark. As for the daylight, he had no idea what he would do.

Maybe he could look at the cliffs. Were they scalable? Could you go down them? Were there any caves? He didn't know, and he certainly would not try it in the dark. Tonight would be a game of survival. A game of hiding out. The night was his cover, and he had to use it. Maybe he could also get hold of Hope.

He had to believe she was still out there. She could handle herself. He realised he was worried, but also incredibly proud of her. She'd seen this coming. Well, something like it, anyway.

He grabbed the bag and threw it over his shoulder, making sure he was zipped up tight, and then began the treacherous scramble around the edge of the shooting range. He looked down towards the pontoon harbour. As far as he could tell, the boat that Geordie had taken had not come back. He couldn't see anyone else at the harbour.

In the darkness and driving rain, he marched across, then down a slope, to arrive eventually at the viewpoint. It was a small shelter, but it had open sides. John could see from it, and yet there was enough wall to hide behind, away from the rain. He took off the backpack and dumped it down. Ian was struggling, so he wrapped him up again and started talking soothingly to him.

He'd need to look down every so often. He'd need to work out how to keep watch. Ian suddenly cried. *Maybe he's hungry*, thought John. *But you can't do that*. He wrapped the surrounding coat tighter. Ian continued crying. John took his little finger and placed it in Ian's mouth. The baby grabbed hold and sucked it.

'That's it,' said John, 'that's it.' He couldn't hear anybody coming, so loud was the rain bouncing off the roof of the viewpoint. 'Quiet,' he said in a whisper to Ian. 'You need to keep quiet till Mum comes. Mum's going to come. Mum's going to make this all right. Dad'll look after you till Mum comes.'

He knew he had to believe it, had to be strong. But he also thought ahead. *If he could get through the night, how did he let anyone know they were in trouble? Hope had said there was the radio. Other systems too. Would there be a boat coming? After all, they had supplies. They came every three days, four days, something like that.*

He reached over and took out a chocolate bar, unwrapped it, and ate it. He could feel the cold, but the coat was good. It was one of those proper mountain ones Hope had told him to get. And he was grateful now. He was sure that Ian was grateful too. The child was snug, held tight in his dad's warmth. He wondered where she was, though. Where was his Hope? And the time spent in that hire car, that first meeting came back to him again. She'd be out there and would be okay. She'd know what to do. He had to believe it. Any other option was not worth thinking about.

Chapter 20

John was okay. Ian was okay. John had got them out. John would keep him safe.

This mantra rolled over Hope's mind repeatedly as she stood at the edge of the structure. The rain was driving down, and she wasn't really equipped to be running around in the cold. Yes, she'd changed clothes, and they had been dry when she put them on, but in truth, if she went out there, she would get soaked so quickly.

However, there were other things to consider. The staff were out hunting for John and her but Hamish was still controlling the game from inside the lounge. Hope had got back close enough to get a view into the lounge. The lights were still on, and she could see a rather unwell Alison Mathers sitting in a seat, but pale white. She could also see Hamish still rambling on, walking around while everyone else was handcuffed.

It had been a while now since it had happened, maybe three hours. Ollie had not been seen, yet he must be searching for her. Hope didn't care. What she did care about was how she was going to rescue these people given the number of hostages and the number of hostage takers. If she could swing the odds even slightly, if she could incapacitate a few and take some guns out of action, there were enough people to bring down this kidnapping. But she needed to work out how to do it.

Part of her just wanted to find John, wanted to be with her little one. But she was a detective inspector, and other people were at risk too; John, at least, had got away. These others were in imminent danger.

She heard somebody moving in her vicinity, so Hope climbed a stanchion, going up onto the roof of the structure. It was slippery, and the rain was driving down, but she laid flat, ignoring the cold. She crawled across until she could look in through a window to the lounge.

Hamish was getting everyone on the move. Using his gun, he got everyone to stand. Alison Mathur swayed, but she got poked with the barrel of the gun. Her daughter screamed and got slapped for it, but Hamish got Stephen Winner to help hold up Alison. They started emptying the lounge, starting a slow walk with Ella leading the hostages.

Hope crawled across the roof to see the pontoon outside the lounge that led to the pods. Ella was there, opening the pod doors using a key card. Ollie wasn't there, but Helena and Christophe were marching the captives along, pushing them into their rooms.

They weren't gentle about it. Alison Mathers, struggling, limping along, was kicked in and Hope noticed Helena spat on her. The group had clearly done something wrong down in Brazil. A wrong that hadn't been put right. A wrong that hadn't received justice, and yet this was wrong too.

And why are we caught up in it? thought Hope. *Why am I here with the rooms all locked?*

Hope saw the pod at the end being opened, with tins of paint were being carried to the lounge by Helena and Christophe.

She wondered what they were doing decorating. *Was this their way of telling everyone what their endgame was? How were they getting out of here?*

Hope thought that she would need to move, for the rain was coming down even harder and she was getting cold—freezing. She needed to do more than move, for she needed shelter. The structure here wouldn't be good for shelter, for how would she hide out in there, when they were all over it?

She made her way back across the roof, dropped and looked at the jetty. *I could take a jet ski, maybe get over to Hirta. It'll be awkward at night, navigation being hard due to those clouds, no stars to navigate by. Might be something for tomorrow.*

She noticed that two of the boats were gone. Had John been stupid enough to go out on a boat in this weather? He wouldn't survive. Her heart sank. John was everything but John didn't have the skills she had. John never had to think about people who could kill. He thought about the people who were trying to get away with not paying. Those who wanted to explain why the dents on the front of the car weren't their fault.

Hope found herself starting to drift and think about him but snapped back quickly. Now was not the time. She had to think about herself and what to do. Hope looked up at Boreray and saw the shooting range. There was the lookout point and the observatory too. *One of those*, she thought. *Go up to one of those. Where would John go?*

She thought he might make for the shooting range because there were weapons there. And if John wasn't there, there were weapons there. She could take one. Hope could fire a gun. Not that she'd done it very often, but she knew how to. She'd also seen plenty of shotguns in her time, knew how to work them, how to load them. It wouldn't be easy, and they had the upper hand in terms of weapons, and she was running out of options.

Hope looked up at the shooting gallery, then stepped out, but not onto the path. Rather, she climbed the hill via the sodden grass beside the path. It was tough going. Her body was frozen. She'd have to get inside and think if she could dry herself. Maybe there were towels up there. This was a special resort, after all. There must be something up there. Showers, maybe. She hoped so. Hope hadn't been up there and had only John's report to go on. He had talked little about the facilities, but more about what had gone on.

Hope continued on up the hill. She glanced behind her several times, but the rain was so heavy, she could barely see anything in the dark, and she certainly wouldn't have heard them. As she reached the shooting range, she cut across in front of the light to make her way round to the door.

Hope pulled it open and closed it behind her. The rain was no longer assaulting her, and she shook herself, almost like a dog, trying to get rid of the drips. She looked around. There were gun cabinets, but they were wide open. She checked, but there was nothing there. She saw the ammunition cupboard, but again there was nothing. There was drink, alcohol, bottles of water and other soft drinks.

As Hope walked over to the drinks, she halted. The water bottles had been disturbed. There were a couple of bottles just lying on the floor. She looked and saw ear defenders as if they'd been dumped on the floor.

Had John been up here? Had John come? Why would he put ear defenders on the floor? Unless he wanted a bag. Of course, she thought. *He's got chocolate, he's got sweets, he's got drink.* Quietly, she called out.

'John, are you here? It's Hope. Are you here?'

There was silence. Her heart sank. She'd hoped he was here, for she could defend him then. Clearly he wasn't. Hope looked around. She'd come here to seek shelter, but also thinking there might be towels. There wouldn't be any over at the viewpoint.

Hope walked along the range to the far end. There was a toilet, and inside it, several towels—hand towels, small, but they would have to do. Hope pulled off her top and hung it over the toilet, reckoning that the dripping into the toilet would be masked by the rain outside. Shaking out her top, she put it to one side and took the towel and dried herself. Her underwear was sodden too, but she kept it on as she dried, trying to make it less damp with the towel.

Hope knew she was exposed here, a tough place to defend with no weapons. And she couldn't see back down the track without going outside. But she also needed to get something to wear, something warmer. Beyond the toilet were a few more cupboards. One was large and tall. She opened it to find a large coat. It was luminous, and she gave a sigh. It wasn't exactly what she wanted.

She pulled it out anyway, though, and turned it inside out, for the interior was dark. There were two jackets, and so she took the first one, now turned inside out, and shoved the arms of the second one into it. The aim was to trap the fluorescence between the two jackets.

Hope tried the creation on, and it seemed to work. It wasn't perfect, but at least she could move in the dark with this. If she went out in the fluorescent jacket, they'd see her in no time, but the darkness of the interior would shield her. The inner jacket would also keep her dry.

Hope placed it down ready for when she wanted to leave. She went back to the toilet and dried her clothes again, but the towels could only take so much before they were wet as well. She shivered and looked around. There was a kettle, and Hope boiled to make a coffee with the little packets left by the kettle.

Hope gratefully took the cup in her hands. It was warm, at least. Hope sipped the coffee and then put her clothes back on. They were damp but no longer sodden. She took the large jacket that she'd created and put it on and continued to drink her coffee. Carefully, she went out to the door. Opening it, she looked down the path and tried to scan the darkness.

Would anybody be coming up to her? Had they searched up here already?

She thought about where John would be. If he'd been here, he wouldn't have been daft enough to be out in this weather. He'd have had to have gone for shelter. Surely, he'd have run for shelter, for he'd have little Ian to look after too.

What did Ian have on? What clothing? He was alive; he had to be alive. Both were. John had got them out; John had got them somewhere.

Her heart said they were alive, but her head was in two minds and kept pointing out that maybe they weren't. Maybe this—maybe that. She cursed her detective brain. You didn't run on optimism when you were solving cases, but then again, it wasn't quite that the people who died didn't matter, but they weren't your own. Yes, you did your damnedest to make sure they were okay, but she never felt about them the way she felt about her two boys.

Hope guessed the closest to this was when Ross got shot. Or when Macleod got attacked. Or when she was attacked.

She thought about what she'd gone through and how John was letting her go back to that life. A dangerous life, and here he was with her. In the middle of it. She should have seen it sooner, though. She told herself she should have seen it coming. Should have got them away.

She reached over and took some chocolate bars, stuffing them in her pockets. She opened one and chewed on it, washing it down with her hot coffee. Hope would have to move. This was not a place you could hide out. Well, you couldn't see anybody coming, and she spent quite a while here. It had been worth it because now she was drier and had a large coat in which she could face the elements.

She had the disappointment of finding there were no weapons here. Finding a weapon, while an option, was not an end-all. She needed to look at how to communicate the problem to the mainland, how to get people to come here. Most importantly, how to get John, Ian, and herself off the island, away from these people.

Yet the detective in her told her she had to stay and rescue the others. Not that many of them were worth it. And then she thought of Laura. She wasn't a bad girl, just mixed up with the wrong type. And then Hope thought again. *Somebody in that group knew about this. It's so well organised,* she thought. *People like Hamish would have no influence on when these people were coming together. Paul had told Laura that he was shocked. And surely that was it. They wouldn't all have come together. There were issues between them. And I've seen that from the fighting that has gone on. What was it all about? Who was at it? Who was the one who brought them together? Who was betraying the group?*

She finished her drink and turned to walk to the front of the range. She'd maybe look out that way, see if she could see the viewpoint. As she went to go, she heard a voice. She could barely make him out. He was in the shadow at the front of the shooting range. Yes, there were lights, but just before the cliff, there was darkness, and the lights inside made it seem even darker out there.

However, the man had raised a shotgun up, and she could see the barrel pointing towards her. 'Adios,' said a voice. It was Ollie's voice. The chef had found her. He'd just said goodbye.

Chapter 21

Hope had nowhere to go. But in those split seconds, the image of Ian ran through her mind. Her little one. She wouldn't see her little one again. Inside, everything went black. Everything churned. And then, she heard a sound.

So quick. So immediate. It was like a whirl. A mechanism being unwound. In the darkness, it was hard to see, but something struck Ollie. And it hit him with such force that he tumbled back. Shotgun wheeling upwards, he fell backwards, straight off the cliff edge.

The driving rain stopped her from hearing his descent. From hearing any splash or a crash off the rocks. One minute the man was there, ready to kill her. The next, he was gone.

Hope stood frozen in disbelief. Someone else was approaching from the front of the range. He had a large coat on and pulled his hood down. Hope saw John. As he stepped inside, she ran to him and flung herself around him. She could see little Ian in the baby carrier beneath the coat. Tears flowed from her eyes. She kissed John. Then she kissed Ian on the head.

'I thought I was gone,' she said. 'I thought I was—'

'I saw you. I saw you come up. It wasn't easy to see. You were in shadow. I decided I would come over, but then I saw him as well. He was sneaking in around the front. So I came in from the other side. I thought I would come up through the trap. Try to surprise him from there. But then he was standing, ready to shoot. I was too far away,' said John, 'so I pulled.' He began to shake.

'Pulled?' asked Hope.

'The button for the mechanism fires the clay pigeons. Very simple mechanism, really. I didn't know how it was set. I just pressed the green button. It fired the clay pigeon, and one of them hit him. He went down,' said John. 'Do you think he's dead?'

'He's dead, John. He's not going to fall off that cliff and survive.'

She saw John's face freeze as he shivered. 'I've never killed anyone,' he said.

'He was going to kill me. You had no option; you did what was right.' John stared into nothing. 'You saved me, you saved me for him,' Hope said pulling John a little closer.

He wasn't used to this sort of situation. Hope realised she, unfortunately, was. She'd seen too many life-and-death moments. Jumping at the dam, detonator in hand. Diving into the water moments when people say you were being heroic but you weren't. You were just acting on instinct. Doing things to save the day. John had done that but had to take a life. She held his face and looked into his eyes. Something had died in there. She kissed him.

'I'm alive because of you,' she said. 'I love you, John.'

Her detective experience came to the fore, and Hope thought about what had just happened. They would know that Ollie had been up here. They would know he'd fallen to his death because the tracker would surely show he was out at sea or further away from the range than he should be.

'We need to move, John.'

'Your world,' he said, almost coldly. 'Your world. What do we do?'

'We need to get away from here. If he's got a tracker on him, they know he's been here, and if he doesn't come back, they'll know we're here. Besides, we can't defend this place. You can't see out of it back down the slope. It's a good shelter, but you can't—'

'I knew that,' said John, almost coming back to life. 'I went to the viewpoint. There's food at the viewpoint.'

Hope stepped over to the door and looked out into the darkness. She could see no one. 'They're putting something together,' she said. 'They've brought the paint out of the other pod. I think they're going to decorate the place. They intend to kill these people, I think. And us with them.'

'Why?' asked John.

'Because of what happened out in Brazil. Some of the workers here are from Brazil. They knew the people who died. They're going to finish them. There's no rescue here. There's nowhere to go.'

'Are we doomed then?' asked John. 'How do we get out of here?'

'Maybe tomorrow we can get on a boat, maybe we can signal. I don't know, but for now we need to hide out. The main structure's not safe to go to.'

'No,' said John.

'How did you get up here, anyway? And how come you have a coat? How did you—?'

John recounted Hamish's coming to their pod. 'I just knew it; something was wrong, very wrong. So, I put a coat on before I went to the lounge. It sounded sensible to Hamish, anyway. We were going to look at the birds, so I packed, getting as prepared as I could. When we were in there, Hamish was so worried about looking for you. Constantly, "Where were you? Where were you?" I just thought,' said John, 'I needed to get out of there. I stepped out quietly, just in time. They shot Alison, didn't they?'

'Hamish had them all taken back to the pods. They've locked them in their pods while they're preparing the place. I don't understand why. There's five of them left. Ollie's gone, but the others are still there. They have weapons. I don't know how to save the rest of them,' said Hope. 'But we need to. We need to work something out.'

'Do we wait until the morning?' asked John.

'I can't take the chance. They could be dead by then. They have a radio. You know how to work a radio, don't you?'

'Probably,' said John.

'Well, maybe you could go. I'll look after Ian. I'll make sure Ian's safe,' said Hope.

'No,' said John. 'I will. You need to do this. Even though you've almost been killed, you need to go. This is your world. You understand it. You understand how to move quietly.'

'Well, you got up here. You got away. You can think like that clearly. I'll look after the wee one. Besides, he's going to need me. He's going to need feeding. He's going to—'

'Hope, look at me. I just killed someone, and I'm frozen. I can't move. Do you think I'm going to take on anyone else?' There were tears in his eyes now.

'I would like to shelter,' said Hope. 'I would like just to bring

Ian and you together with me and protect you through the night. But if we don't do something, these people are going to be dead. I need to go to the radio. It was switched off, but I think it could work. I saw how to get the aerial up. I saw how to call the Coastguard. He took me through that.'

'Then he'll know that,' said John.

'He will, which is why I have to go now. I have to go now while it might still be there.'

'I'll take Ian. We'll go to the lookout. We'll stay there,' said John.

Hope grabbed him and held him tight. She kissed him again and again. 'Stay safe,' she said.

'Don't die yourself,' said John. 'I won't be coming with you this time. I won't be there to save you.'

She kissed him again on the forehead. 'I'll be back. I've got this one to feed, anyway.'

They both exited through the front of the shooting range, Hope descending the hill in darkness, John making his way back to the lookout post. As Hope went down the hill, she scanned in front of her, but she could see no one.

Arriving close to the structure, she noted that the boat was back. One rowing boat. She snuck along the pontoon and then up close to the structure, looking into the lounge. There was paint being daubed on the walls. The writing was in a foreign language, but Hope counted who was in.

Hamish was there directing things; Geordie and Ella were also there. Christophe was over towards the door that led to the pods, and Helena was guarding the door that Hope was near. Maybe they didn't know about how she could move under the structure.

That was how she would get to the radio room. There was

no other way in reality. She could climb up on the roof, but she couldn't go right over the top. It was too awkward to get up there to the helipad without going round the back. Besides, with the way the wind was blowing, she didn't want to go up on that roof again.

Hope walked further out to the shed that stood on the pontoon near the boats. She stripped off her clothes, right down to her underwear, and then descended into the sea. It was dark underneath, with no light, and she navigated, hanging on to pontoon edges and then via the pipework as she went under the structure. As long as she got out to the other side, she'd be fine.

Once again there was about a head's worth of space allowing her to breathe as she made her way along. The water, however, was freezing. For the second time tonight, she was chilled to the bone. That would be a problem when she came out, getting dry. But she'd have to make do.

After getting underneath the structure and out the other side, Hope clambered up onto the pontoon where the supply boats arrived. Carefully, she made her way to the door at the rear. Nowhere seemed to be locked down, and Hope entered the corridor for the radio room without incident. She padded along, realising she'd leave wet footprints.

But she could hear them. Hamish and his cohorts were shouting and getting on as if they'd won something. It was the euphoria of a plan coming together. Clearly, they weren't worried about Hope and John. They didn't know her profession, and she was so glad of that right now. But then again, Ollie was out dealing with them. Maybe they hadn't realised he'd met his end. *Poor John*, thought Hope. But he'd saved her. He'd saved her.

Hope stepped into the radio room and looked in dismay. The place was a mess. Wires had been pulled. Units had been smashed. There was nothing here. Nothing here to use. They'd gone completely incommunicado. She thought for a moment.

The *supply vessel comes tomorrow or their vessel. Whatever it is, it will come to take them away. But if it does, who would be on it? Would the guests be taken away? Is that why they were leaving Hope and John, as they were unimportant?*

So far, everyone had been put back in their pods, but Hope's mind said one creator was on the inside. There was no way Hamish could have organised all of this. Somebody knew the details about the guests, had influence over their diaries.

Taking a last look at the radio room, scanning for any sort of short-distance radio, anything that she could use, she found nothing. She would have to move quickly. They were all still in the lounge area, but if they found her, she was in no state to mount any sort of defence.

Chilled to the core, still in her underwear, Hope got back into the water and made her way back underneath the structure. When she came out the other side, she climbed into the shed and found a piece of rag to dry herself down as best she could. She was still damp when she put her clothes back on, including the large protective jacket combination, and then snuck away back onto Boreray.

In the darkness, she climbed up to the lookout point. John had seen her coming, and when she got inside, he hugged her. She was shaking, her teeth chattering. He opened up his coat and lay down. Hope took hers off and clambered inside his before letting hers fall over them. Ian was trapped in the middle, and he whimpered for his mother.

'He's hungry,' said John. 'He's been looking for you.'

Hope lifted her top and allowed Ian to feed, but John still kept her in a hug. He passed her chocolate, and she ate until she felt she might be sick, but she ate and drank from John's rescued bottles of water.

'I'm not sure they'll care about us,' said Hope. 'The radio's gone. It's wrecked. There's nowhere we can go.'

'So what?' said John. 'What do we do?'

'We can't do anything tonight. In the morning, I'll go look. In the morning, I'll make a plan. Work out what we're going to do. And then we'll need to get help or to end this.'

She looked down at the wee one and then over at John and smiled. 'We're still here,' she said. 'We're still alive.' John stood up and placed the coat combinations around Hope.

'You rest,' he said. 'I'll watch the path. Make sure no one's coming. You need to sleep. Need to get warm.'

He stood looking out, and she could tell from his face that something had changed. There was a hardness there that she had never known in him. She had thought it wasn't in him.

He's just killed someone to save me. And he's probably wondering if he's going to have to kill anyone else. And he's still here and not falling apart.

She held little Ian tight, thankful that, for now, her family were still together.

Chapter 22

'Have you been there all night?'

John looked down from his post. The day was just beginning, with the sun breaking over the horizon. 'I let you sleep. You needed it. Are you any warmer?'

Hope shook her head. 'I still feel chilled. But obviously, it must not have been too bad. I must have had some heat in here. The wee man helps.'

'You slept through,' said John. 'I could tell. I can always tell when you're sleeping. I've watched you enough.'

'You watch me when I sleep.'

'I watch you a lot.'

'Are you holding up?'

'I'm okay,' said John, in a completely unconvincing voice.

'You had to do it. You had to.'

'Don't,' said John. 'Just don't. We must focus. We have to do what's here and now. I can't think about stuff. I need to just get on with it.'

Hope understood. Many a time in her job, she had to push back what was happening, the thoughts running through her head, just to keep going. The horror she saw. And this was a horror for John. It was a horror that he'd had to instigate, albeit to save her.

She reached over and took a chocolate bar and handed it to him. 'Make sure you eat,' she said. 'I understand. Push it back. Until we get away from here, we push it back. But at some point, you'll have to deal with it. And we will. We'll deal with it together. But for now, eat.'

John took the chocolate bar and wolfed it down. He then took water from Hope and drank that as well. Hope drank plenty because she needed to. Trying to reconcile being a mother, and a feeding mother, alongside trying to be the hero and rescue people, was all becoming a little absurd. But here they were, trapped so far out. She needed to get up and find out what was going on.

'I'm going to scout,' said Hope. 'You stay here with Ian. If anybody comes, do what you need to do.'

'Are there any caves down the side here?'

'It's sheer,' said Hope. 'And trying to climb down something like that, even if there was a cave, would be suicide. If you see somebody coming, stay low. If they're coming towards you, get away. Go into the observatory. Go hide somewhere.'

John nodded and waited until Hope got up and passed little Ian over to him. He put the baby carrier on, leaving Ian wrapped up inside his coat.

'I'll be back,' said Hope. 'I'm just scouting. I won't be taking anyone on. It seems they've given up on us. I don't think we matter.'

'I don't think anybody matters to them,' said John. His tone was down. Hope didn't like it. He needed to be positive. He needed to see success. She needed a plan. Hope needed to give John something he could hold on to.

'I'll be back shortly,' she said. Hope was aware that in daylight going down the grass they could possibly see her as she came down, but she was banking on the fact that they wouldn't be that bothered. She walked along Boreray and made her way up first to the shooting range. Carefully she entered, making sure no one was there, and then began hunting again until she came up with what she wanted. A pair of binoculars. They were good ones too, for nothing was skimped on here. She exited the shooting range and started descending the side of Boreray until she could see the pods.

Through the binoculars, she could see the captives in their pods. The pods had a terrific view of the sea, but Boreray stretched just far enough that at its edge you could see the pod windows. However, Hope was right on a cliff edge and had climbed down some rocks to obtain her viewing position.

Alison Mathers was lying down on her bed. Her daughter seemed in tears. There was Paul and Laura, Laura looking distraught, but they were separated within the pod at present. Paul seemed to be aloof. Meanwhile, Federico and Maisie were holding each other, clearly terrified. Stephen and Tammy were arguing about something, while Terence and Alicia sat beside each other, looking very grim-faced. Corey Denman was banging on the door of his pod, shouting, while Sylvia was on the floor, crying.

Sylvia thought Hope, *she's an innocent. Laura's an innocent. The wives may be innocent. Are they going to kill everyone? What were they going to do?*

She focused on the rest of the structure. There was Geordie tying something around different stanchions. Ella was helping him. Hamish was marching back and forward, and when she looked inside the lounge, she could see that they'd gone to town the previous night. There was so much put up on the walls. She saw posters. What looked like a village? She was just too far away to get the exact details.

They were leaving a mural of sorts. Was that the plan? Kill everybody off? Leave a mural? Would it matter? Would Hope and John matter? Or were they just biding their time to finish them? Were they going to blow people up?

That's what it looked like with the stanchions being attended to. It could be explosives they were attaching. Hope couldn't see clearly enough, and she would not get too close. If they were leaving John and her alone at the moment, that was good. And she didn't want to provoke them. They surely weren't doing a suicide pact. They wouldn't kill themselves as well. That would be, well, for what purpose?

There was the clanging thought that said somebody, somebody who bought this place, somebody who funded it, was in on this. She thought there was no way Hamish could have pulled this off, being employed. Too much of a coincidence. Too much to get all his people in the right place.

Somebody would have to pull strings for that. Most of these people wouldn't care. They'd fund the project, and then that would be it. But somebody had to run the project. Somebody had to be over the top on it. Somebody had to be taking an interest. Who was it? Who had pulled them all together in the same place at the same time?

She sighed, turned, and made her way back across Boreray. When she did so, she found John wasn't there. A moment's panic leapt into her until she looked across towards the observatory, and he was walking his way back. When he arrived, she looked at him.

'You said you were going to stay here.'

'There's a boat coming,' he said. 'It's out there. You can see it with the observatory telescope. I had to point it down, but I saw it.'

'So, is it coming to take them away?' asked Hope. 'Will they leave us here?'

'We know everybody, don't we?' said John.

'They're all known, anyway. There must be employment records.'

'So, what do they intend to do? Just die here?'

'They might set up a tall tale to cover their tracks, say that somebody came in and did this. And then those who are left behind put their hands up and say, "We were victims, but they left us because we were just the staff." Or "We escaped,"' said Hope. 'That would be one way to play it. But that would mean they'd have to come for us because we know the truth.'

'So why are they waiting? Why aren't they finishing us?' asked John.

'Maybe they've got more people coming on this boat. Maybe they don't see the need at nighttime to have come for us. But now, when the others arrive, maybe they'll come then.'

'What are they doing down there, though?' asked John.

'Well, they're attaching stuff to the stanchions. I think they're explosives. I think they're just going to blow them up in their pods.'

'No,' said John.

'What do you mean, no?'

'This trouble in Brazil—it was a collapse, yes?' Hope nodded. 'Why would you blow them up? What would blowing them up signify? You could hang them and say they were wicked people. That would signify something. But blowing them up, no. I think they're going to sink them.'

'What?' blurted Hope.

'They're going to sink them. I think they'll blow the structure and let the pods descend into the water. They'll die; they'll suffocate. Those people who were in the collapse must have suffocated. They must have felt the horror of everything coming down on them. That's what they're doing,' said John.

For a moment, Hope felt pride in him. If she'd been sitting in the station in Inverness and one of her team had said this, as grim as it was, she'd have felt pride. But this was John having to identify a horror. He shouldn't be here; he shouldn't have to do this. This was not his place. And when he said it, he didn't have the satisfaction that a detective had. Yes, it was horrible, but you'd cracked it. Instead, it was only horror that filled his face. He couldn't ride that professional pride, the one you had to have despite the horror of the circumstances, the one that kept you going.

'So, what's our plan?' he asked.

'The boat,' said Hope. 'If the boat's coming, that's their get-out-of-here plan. If we take the boat, they've nowhere to go. They're trapped. The boat will also have DSC, a way to call the Coast Guard. It'll have EPIRBs, floating devices that send a message to satellites when a distress situation occurs. We need to get the message out that something's wrong here. We need to get more forces on our side.'

'And the only way to do that,' said John, 'is that boat. They've destroyed everything here, haven't they?'

'Yes,' said Hope. 'Yes, it's set up as a place to get away from it all. So, the only communication, the only place you can get hold of the outside world, is at the rear of that structure, in the radio room, and they have destroyed it. I presume it was there until late, because they needed to contact the ship and make sure it was on time. Now, there's no need. So, they wrecked it. It also means if they couldn't get us and had to leave, there'd be no time frame for us to catch them. They'd be away. We couldn't communicate with anyone. We'd have to survive here until somebody came and found us.'

'You stay here with Ian,' said Hope. 'When the boat comes, I will go. I'll try to infiltrate it. I'll get on board and take it over, get a message away. You stay out here with Ian. You keep him away.'

'No,' said John.

'What do you mean, no? We can't put him at risk.'

'He's been at risk since the moment they started this,' said John. 'And if you go for that boat and it doesn't work, what then? Then I have to do it with him. No, I'll hold him. I'll take care of him, but I know how to sail a ship, remember?'

She hadn't remembered. She'd been seeing John all along as a person to protect, not an asset. It was natural, of course. He was her man. He was carrying her little one. So therefore, he was the public to be protected. In fact, he was more than the public to be protected. He was everything to be protected. But John stood looking at her with a sharp intensity in his eyes that she didn't know.

'If we're going to get through this,' he said, 'we need to take that boat. You and me. And yes, the little one with us. Can't leave him down anywhere. He's too small. Can't come back for him. Growing up, I sailed boats. I know how to handle them, always have. If we can take the vessel, I can get us home on it. It's how it has to be.'

She reached over and took his hand. 'When we go for it, we go for it. You can't worry about me. We have to work out what we're going to do, and then we have to do it. If something happens to me, you have to keep going.'

'I want my partner and my child,' said John. 'I will keep going.

I will keep going until this is done.'

Hope gave him a smile, but underneath she was worried about him. He was beyond himself in an impossible situation. John had no training and no way of coping except to focus his anger, to use it. She had to make him have a plan and follow it. And he was right. He would be a great asset to her.

On her own, taking out that many people was impossible. She wasn't Kirsten. She wished she were. If Kirsten were here, this whole thing could be sorted in a couple of minutes. She was Service-trained. Hope wasn't, but she had training. The police work had given her some things. She just prayed it was enough.

Chapter 23

Hope watched the ship approach the main structure. The rain had stopped, and it was now blustery, a cold, crisp day, out in the middle of nowhere. John had the binoculars and was scanning the ship as best he could.

'How many can you see?' asked Hope.

'Two on deck,' said John. 'Obviously somebody's steering it. Other than that, I have seen no one.'

'Well, we'll wait until it docks.'

'But what if they don't come off? What if Hamish and his crew just walk straight onto the boat and leave?'

'Then that's what they do,' said Hope. 'Our best chance is to sneak on while some of them are on shore. If Hamish is just going to step on board and set off an explosion of some sort from the boat, well then, honestly, John, we're stuffed. But I don't see that they can do that. They must come for us. Otherwise, we know the complete story. We'll be able to tell that someone at the top was involved.'

'But they don't know that,' said John. 'They don't know that you know that, or at least you suspect that.'

'They'll come. They'll clean up. You can't leave loose ends. I think somebody's going to survive whatever they are going to do. And they're going to have to take him away.'

'Or her,' said John. 'Alison Mathers got shot in the foot. Doesn't mean she wasn't involved. It's a great way to turn around and say, "It wasn't me."'

'You've been watching too many detective programmes,' said Hope. 'There's few of them who would take a bullet just to prove their innocence. There's not that many who would buy somewhere like this just to satisfy a wrong.'

'I disagree with that. And besides, they got everybody else to buy into it. It's not all their money. It's somebody else's too.'

They watched from the lookout until the boat came in and tied up. A couple of people got off at the pontoon, met by Hamish, and then disappeared inside of the structure.

'What do you see?' asked Hope. 'Anybody else on that boat?'

'There's at least one, no, maybe two.'

'Okay,' said Hope. 'So, we need to sneak on, but it's at the rear of the structure. We might have to go in via the water,' said Hope.

'That's all right for you,' said John. 'I can't go in via the water. I can't go in with a little guy. He'd be soaked, freeze to death, even if we kept ourselves alive.'

Hope wondered for a moment. She looked down at the structure. The rear side, where the vessel was docked, was difficult to get to. You could walk through the structure, but that wasn't workable, given that Hamish and his goons were inside. You could go underneath, and Hope could manage that, but John wouldn't be able to do that. The only other option was to go across the roof, where you would be seen on a day like this.

Or there was the possibility of going around the side. There didn't seem to be that much to hang on to. She'd be asking

John to clamber around the side of a structure, and indeed at one point, by the looks of it, walk across a pipe. A pipe that was at least twenty feet high in the air. He'd have to do that with a baby carrier on, and nothing to support him.

'Well, what do you see?' asked John.

'I could go in underneath by the water. That could surprise them. Come up the side of the boat. The only way I can see to get you there is to go around the side.'

'But there isn't anything at the side to cling on to. Not once you start. I'd get about twenty feet,' said John, 'and then there's only that pipework going across.'

'The pipework that you're going to have to shimmy across.'

'What? Sit on and then shuffle across,' said John. 'That won't work, will it? I'll be a sitting duck.'

'What's the other option?' asked Hope. 'Run across?'

'Run across?' queried John. 'I'll have to run across?'

'No,' said Hope. 'If you fall, you'll end up in the water. Then they'll hear you and just shoot you. It's too great a risk.'

'You said they're going to come and hunt us down. That's your belief,' said John. 'At which point does anything not become too much of a risk? When is it not going to be okay to do this? That's the only way I'll get over. We've already said, if we go underneath, Ian will freeze.'

'We could hold him above our heads.'

'How difficult is going underneath?' asked John. 'Do you think you could seriously hold him up while clambering under?'

'No,' said Hope. 'And you don't swim the way I do either. No, it's not safe for you going underneath.'

'Then I'll go at the side. If we both come from different places, if one of us gets spotted, at least the other one's got a chance to help them out.'

'Good idea,' said Hope. 'But let's move. We don't know how long they're going to spend here. How long before they come for us.'

Hope ditched the fluorescent jackets she'd been wearing, leaving them behind. It wasn't warm, but she wasn't soaking wet like the night before. The clothes had dried in the wind, and although she still felt the chill, and soon would do when she got into the water, she was also beginning to feel more pumped up. She saw an end game in this. A chance to finish it. That was more important than anything else. It was a chance to get her little one off this rock. A chance for them all to go home.

John, however, kept his large coat on, with Ian attached by the baby carrier. He needed to protect the child. He wasn't sure that the child would stay warm enough. Luckily, his jacket wasn't fluorescent.

The pair crept down towards the complex, Hope going first and then waving John on. They seemed to have been forgotten, almost ignored. Maybe there was a plan for them, but maybe that plan was to be enacted later.

She thought about it from Hamish's perspective. They could spend hours trying to hunt down Hope and John, when really, they wanted to get it done and get out of there. Whatever they were going to do, once it was done, they could pull the people who were involved in it into the hunt for Hope and her family. Boreray was not large, and hunting them down would not be difficult.

They got close to the structure, and Hope pointed to John, showing him where he would jump on at the side. It was out of view of anyone, but once he ran across the pipe, he'd be in view until he got to the other side. The pipe was not that wide. You could straddle it with your legs, but you were in full view of a gallery, a gallery that no one was in currently.

John started off, and Hope grabbed his hand. 'Be careful. If anything goes wrong, get into the water. Just get back up and out of here. Route back up to the viewpoint.'

'See you on the other side,' he said.

He gave a smile, but underneath she knew he was all determination, all anger pointed at getting to the other side to deal a blow to these people. Hope watched as he climbed up, little Ian strapped in front of him. John was quickly clambering across and then was standing up on the pipe, his hands held out for balance. He was still out of view of the gallery, and he turned to give Hope a wave, waiting for her to give the okay for him to run across the pipe.

Just as he did so, Hope saw someone walking through the gallery. She put her hand up, telling him to halt. He crouched back down again, making his balance much easier.

Hope waited for five minutes. It was Geordie, and who knew what he was doing? It was as if he was admiring the scenery, but then he had a spray can and was painting something on the window. Then he disappeared.

Hope waved her hand, and John stood up. His arms went to either side, and he bolted. She saw him halfway across, going well, and then one foot seemed to slip. He hammered down the other foot, but stumbled, and then made a desperate dive. Her heart was in her mouth as he tumbled forward, but his hands reached and clung onto a small pipe that was on the other side of the structure.

She watched as he tried to swing himself up. John was in decent shape, but he wasn't the most athletic person. He must have been running on sheer adrenaline as he hauled himself up, carefully trying not to crush Ian, and got to the other side.

He gave a thumbs up, but she could tell he was winded, if not sore, from the dive. Hope dropped straight away into the water by the pontoons. It took her five minutes to go underneath and negotiate her way until she came up on the pontoon where the ship had docked. Hope looked across the pontoon and could see John looking out from the side of the complex. She put her thumb up, and he clambered down onto the pontoon.

Hope rolled herself up onto it, and they set off quickly, coming alongside the vessel. Hope stepped on board and went around to the aft of the vessel and almost ran into someone with a gun. She stepped past, put her arm around the man's throat, and slapped her other hand over his mouth. What she did next wasn't pretty, but it was effective, as she turned him, pulling with her arm, and drove his head into a metal stanchion. The man went out like a light, and she dropped him to the floor.

Hope picked up the gun, looked at it, made sure the safety was off, and then walked down the corridor, inside the vessel. She could hear a brief commotion and wondered what was going on. But she crept along the side of the vessel, where the corridor ran.

A door opened in front of her, and she drove the butt of the gun into a man's face. He fell to the ground, and she hit him again on the head. He had now fallen and the door crushed against him. Although the man was clearly unconscious, if anyone came down the stairs, they'd see him. She bent down, trying to fold his legs away, and then she heard the sound from the stairs. A man was coming down. He arrived, gun in his hand, and saw her.

There was a moment of shock between the two of them. Then, a fire extinguisher went off in his face. The white carbon dioxide layered in a foam across him, and he was then clunked in the back of the head by the fire extinguisher. Hope heard a child begin to cry and saw John standing there holding the fire extinguisher.

She couldn't deal with Ian now. She had to get up towards the bridge. Quickly she ran, holding the gun in front of her, but there was no one else on board. The bridge was clear, and she told John to stand guard on it. Then she ran down, checking every compartment. The ship was empty.

Hope untied the ropes that held the ship to the pontoon. When she jumped back on board, she joined John on the bridge. He set off the ship's DSC, the Digital Selective Calling, that would send an SOS message out to all the ships in the vicinity. Not that there were many nearby. She saw John locate the EPIRB, an electronic device that, when submerged in the water, would send off a satellite signal declaring distress. She watched him detach it and sling it overboard. It was then that she heard the plane.

'Have they got somebody watching them?' asked Hope, her heart in her mouth.

'No,' said John, 'that's the fishery protection aircraft. It was out here the other day.'

Hope watched him looking around the ship, and then he ran below deck before returning and stepping just outside the bridge, something in his hands.

'What's that you've got?'

'Signal lamp,' said John. He pointed it up at the aircraft and flashed a message.

'What are you telling them?'

'SOS,' said John. 'What else is there?'

He watched as the aircraft came back and circled again. John kept the message going, and again the aircraft turned and flew low over them. He waved as it passed less than fifty feet above. It seemed to waggle its wings, an acknowledgement, and then circled above again.

Hope smiled at John. She reached out with her hand, but an explosion rang out. The force was so strong that the structure was clearly shaking.

'We need to get out of here,' said John.

He grabbed the controls of the ship and began backing it away from its mooring, before turning and powering it away from the structure. From the rear, nothing could be seen, but smoke was pouring from the front of the structure. John opened up the throttle, and while keeping a distance, he steered round to the front. Hope gasped.

The pods at the front had become detached and had begun to sink into the water. John had been right. They'd blown off the stanchions around the pods. The pods were sinking. Through the large windows, Hope could see the guests screaming. *Couldn't they open the pods?* It appeared not. The water inside was rising.

'Get close,' said Hope.

As she said it, a bullet hole exploded in the window at the front of the vessel. She glanced over and saw Hamish and his goons firing, clearly intent on pushing the ship away.

'What do we do?' cried Hope. 'How are we going to get them out?'

'We'll have to get close, but I don't know how we get them out.'

'Well, think, John, think,' shouted Hope, 'because we've got to do something.'

Chapter 24

'Right, brace,' said John. 'Just brace.'

'Brace for what?' said Hope.

'Impact!'

John had opened up the throttle on the boat again and was now racing towards the pod structure. It was descending, with more than half of each pod underneath the water. But John went full tilt with the boat, ramming into one pod. It split, cracking apart, and Hope dived off the boat into the water.

The water was chaos. Bubbles everywhere, but she could just about make out the structure. It was daytime now, and although the sea was always blurred to look through, it was at least now much clearer. She swam towards the opening in the pod which the boat had caused. Water was flooding in, and two figures were submerged inside the pod.

She reached in with a hand and felt someone grab hers. Pulling hard, they came out. Letting them go up to the surface, she reached in for the next person. Having grabbed them, Hope kicked hard and broke the surface of the water. Shots rang down around her, but she could see Alison Mathers and her daughter beside her and screamed at them to go for the boat.

The boat was turning now, allowing the women to swim around the aft, protecting them from the gunshots. John, once he'd manoeuvred the boat, now left the helm and ran down to drag them in from the side of the vessel.

'There's more down there,' said Hope.

'Careful,' said John, 'it'll start taking you down with it.'

'I've got to try,' she said.

And with that, she was gone. Hope dived and kicked hard, swimming towards the pod structure. But now, it was full of water, and it was sinking. She could see some blurred faces pressed up against the pod windows, but she couldn't reach them. It tilted, one pod rising slightly, while the rest of it swung underneath. The pod window which came up, had a face on it, and also a dent on the side. Hope swam quickly and broke the surface.

'John, I need a bar. I need something to prise with. A jack, anything.'

John ran around the vessel, and returned, throwing her an iron bar. *It's strong enough*, Hope thought. The bar looked like a stanchion for ropes that protected you from going overboard. Whatever it was, it would be worthwhile, and she dived with it, back down to the pod.

But the pod was descending, and Hope struggled. She reached the pod, drove in the metal, and tried to prise it open. Running out of breath, she pressed hard. There wasn't much room, but a small gap opened in the dent, and a hand came through it. Hope pulled, dragging a woman out. But the woman got stuck.

Hope continued to pull, the structure still descending, her lungs beginning to burst. Then, there was blood in the water. The woman was suddenly free, and Hope watched as another hand came out. The pod descended suddenly, and she had to kick hard to get up and break the surface, hearing a shout from John.

She was a little way off the boat now, but it was coming towards her, the aft swinging around. Emily Mathers, Alison's daughter, was there with a helping hand, but Hope pushed the other woman up she had rescued. She realised now it was Sylvia and blood was pouring from her back, a large gouge. It must have been from when she came through the gap, the ragged metal of the small gap cutting into her back.

Hope could see John was on the radio, and the fisheries protection aircraft was still in attendance up above. She lay on the deck as the boat pulled away from the structure, but as it did so, she saw a hand in the water.

'John, John out there, in the water.'

He saw it and turned the vessel. The potshots were still coming from Hamish and his goons. He brought the boat close by the hands in the water. Hope could see there were now four hands, and a couple of heads bobbing up. Together with Emily, she pulled Laura onto the boat along with Paul.

'How'd you get out?' gasped Hope.

'The emergency door,' said Laura, half choking. 'It blew open. Our door . . . the emergency door blew open.'

Laura threw her arms around Hope, hugging her, and Hope felt the boat swing away again. John took the boat to a position a half a mile away from the structure and sat watching it.

'We just wait,' said John. 'I've spoken to the Fisheries Protection Aircraft. They're relaying a message. I've asked them to bring the military. Told him to inform Macleod as well, or at least get hold of the police.'

Hope walked up to the helm and gave John a hug. She looked

down at her little one. He was fast asleep. 'You're telling me he wasn't awake during any of that?' said Hope.

'No,' laughed John. 'No, he wasn't. What do we do now?'

'Maybe we'll just stay here,' said Hope.

'Look,' said Paul, pointing back to the structure. 'They must know what's up.'

Hamish was waving at them, and the guns were now on the ground.

'Well, that's fine,' said Hope. 'We can just wait here.'

'No, we should apprehend them, in case they spin some other sort of story,' said Paul.

'Well, I think their story is all over the structure,' said Hope.

'No, no. They know they're trapped now. I think we can make a deal with them.'

'Make a deal,' said Hope. 'You've got dead people down there.'

'Listen to Paul,' said Laura. 'I mean, he knows what he's about. He's handled big things before.'

Hope thought for a moment. 'Yes,' she said, 'of course. But I don't think we should get too close. We should negotiate with him first.'

'Of course,' said Paul. 'We'll be clever about this. Get your partner to bring the boat round. We'll go close, but not actually to the pontoon at the rear. That way, we can talk to them without being right beside them. And we'll tell them, no guns. They're going to have to put the guns on the ground.'

'Okay,' said Hope. She turned and looked at Sylvia. Blood was still pouring out of her back. 'Turn over,' said Hope, and disappeared off to get the first aid box. As she did so, she also ran over to the helm. 'Do as Paul says,' said Hope, 'but don't let this boat get close enough that Hamish or anyone else can get on board. Any sign of trouble, pull away. Until those guns are on the ground and those people are apprehended, don't dock.'

'Why are we docking anyway? Why are we going anywhere near it?' asked John.

'Trust me,' said Hope, 'just trust me.'

She turned and spent the next five minutes attaching bandages to Sylvia's back. Hope told Emily to keep the pressure on and to keep Sylvia talking. She also told John to get on the radio to advise that they needed more than just military. Medical help was also required. He advised that he'd already asked for that, given what had happened, and Hope gave him a grin. He was doing so well, but she went back to kneel beside Sylvia until the boat came into position.

Hamish was on the pontoon, and Paul went to the foredeck of the boat. Hope stayed close, so she could hear him.

'They will come for us,' said Hamish. 'Maybe we can talk.'

'Maybe we can,' said Paul, 'but all the weapons need to come here first.'

'I will bring them to the pontoon,' said Hamish. 'You can come ashore and inspect them.'

'That's not wise, Paul,' said Hope. 'Better if they threw them onto the end of the boat or put them all in a big bag that they can then throw onto the boat, and we can sort them.'

'I know how to handle a weapon,' said Paul. 'Your partner doesn't; he was rubbish with the shotguns.'

'Okay,' said Hope. She watched as Hamish disappeared and came back with his entire crew. They had a bag, purported to be full of the weapons. John got the boat close, and with a large heave-ho, the bag was thrown onto the deck. Paul went to open it up, but Hope stepped forward.

'I'll do that,' she said.

'You're just a housewife.'

'Detective Inspector Hope McGrath, Police Scotland,' she said. 'I'll inspect the weapons.' She undid the bag with Paul standing behind her.

'Probably best if you give me one,' he said, 'just so I can keep it trained on them, in case they get too close. Hamish. You and the rest lie down, face flat, arms behind your back.'

Hope reached in amongst the weapons and checked them, handing one over to Paul. 'Keep it trained on them in case they move.'

Alison Mathers wandered up to the foredeck of the boat. 'What's going on?'

'They want to make a deal,' said Paul.

'There's no point in making a deal. These people tried to kill us. We need to throw the book at them.'

'Look at it,' said Paul, 'look at it. When the authorities come, they'll see everything they're complaining about. We'll be ruined. We'll be ruined because the story will be out. They'll find out all about what Corey did. How he bribed officials.'

'And what? What can we do now? You've got a detective inspector here.'

'Not for long,' said Paul. He turned and pointed his gun at Hope. 'While you were a housewife, I might even have thought about buying you off. But no, you're just going to be a complication. You too, Alison. But then again, unlike her, you deserve it.'

The man pulled the trigger, pointing the gun at Hope. But Hope stood calmly. There was a click, but there was no gunshot. No bullet.

'Unlike your one,' said Hope, standing up with a gun, 'this one's loaded.'

'What's going on?' said Alison. 'He tried to kill me. Why

would he try to kill me?'

'Because he's behind it all,' said Hope. 'He was the one who brought you all here. He's the one who organised this. And he is the one who was going to walk off. He couldn't live with it. He struggled with what you did. But instead of calling you out there, he listened to what the people said in Brazil. He listened to their stories. He listened to how they died. And he tried to recreate that. And he got most of you,' said Hope. 'And to deflect attention, he was going to kill me as well. I was meant to go down there. Tragic accident. Except it wouldn't be. Hamish and his crew had plastered the story everywhere. What was it to be, John? A terrorist group comes in from the side, that then clears off and you were lucky enough to be picked up by the supply vessel? Was that the idea? Laura wouldn't have made it, would she?'

'Good God,' said Alison Mathers. She walked up to Paul who glared at her. 'You just let them die. You took no responsibility.'

'On your knees,' said Hope. When he did so, she found some rope on deck and tied his hands up behind his back. 'People are on their way,' she said. 'Hopefully, they'll get here in time for Sylvia. Until then, we wait. We won't go ashore, and Paul here will be kept under gunpoint. Take a seat, Alison. Be thankful your daughter's still with you.'

She turned around and shouted over to the helm. 'John, take us out a little. Not too far. Keep working, Emily,' she shouted. 'Keep the pressure on.'

Hope sucked in a deep breath. She'd done it. They would go home. She almost felt a tear in her eye, for she wanted to get home, back to their flat. She wanted to be back in that bedroom, Ian lying in her arms, John holding her. But for now, she'd have to stand a little longer in the cold, and keep her gun trained on someone.

Chapter 25

Hope had watched the helicopters arrive. The first one to set down was the Coastguard, and Hope had kept her gun trained while the paramedic came and saw to the wounded on the boat. Talking through John on the radio, the Coastguard dropped their man directly onto the ship and then took away Sylvia. She was in a bad way.

After they did so, the military arrived. Several helicopters set down personnel on the structure. Hope identified herself, and the military rounded up the offenders, taking everyone inside. Hope could see the story of the collapse at Campo Bonito. There were horrific pictures. People died underneath all of it. And yet, these people had just done the same thing. Hope felt no remorse for any of them, except maybe for those innocents who died at Campo Bonito. Her family had been put at risk, and for what?

Macleod arrived shortly after. Hope didn't know how he swung getting onto a military helicopter, but he spoke with the authority of the police.

'Are you all okay?' asked Macleod as he saw her.

'I'm fine,' said Hope. 'I'm fine.' It felt as if she was in work mode until Macleod threw his arms around her and held her tight.

'Thank God. Thank God.' He then turned to see John in the corner with little Ian. Macleod strode over. 'Good to see you, John,' he said. 'And you,' he said, picking up the child. Macleod held little Ian tight. 'Oh dear God, thank you, thank you, God,' he said out loud. He kissed the child on the top of his head and handed him back to John. 'You've done well,' said Macleod, 'whatever's gone on.'

'Go talk to her,' said John. He was shaking, then held his child, wrapping him up in an enormous hug and looked at no one.

Macleod turned back to Hope. 'Is he okay?'

'No. Last night, someone put a gun on me, ready to kill me. He hit them with, well, with a clay pigeon. The man fell off a cliff. John killed him to save me. I think he's going to need some help with that,' said Hope.

'I'm sorry,' said Macleod. 'We'll get him everything. We'll get whatever you need. But what's gone on?' he said, looking around.

Hope ran through with Macleod all that had happened. 'The picture's on the wall. It's a place called Campo Bonito in Brazil. The people I was here with ran companies that worked there. They killed people because of their neglect, due to what their companies did. But one man, Corey, an American government official, he nullified the criminal neglect proceedings by bribery. He basically told me so.

'The staff who were here came from Brazil, from around that area. Paul, one of the CEOs involved with the companies, brought them here to do this. He organised his fellow investors to all be here at the same time, and he sought to kill them all.'

'What did you have to do with it?' asked Macleod.

Hope looked at him, and her eyes were wild. 'He would have killed me, my son and my partner as collateral, just to show it was something different, just so people wouldn't trace what he was doing. He tried to kill us,' said Hope. Paul was across the room under an armed guard. 'That girl over there,' said Hope, 'Laura is his girlfriend. She was his ex-girlfriend. He brought her back. He would have left her too. She was to be expendable. They were in the only pod on which the emergency doors worked when the pods fell off the front of the structure.'

'The pods,' said Macleod. 'What pods?' Hope took him to the door and showed him the pontoon where the structure had been blown away.

'Everyone was in their pods. They were beautiful, Seoras. An enormous window on the front. You could see the sea, could open it up. You could feel everything. Beautiful. But it was a cell. They locked the pods. Everyone in their pods, and blew them into the sea. We were just fortunate.'

'How are you fortunate? What did you do?'

'The nose kicked into overdrive,' said Hope. 'I had that feeling. You know the feeling.' Macleod nodded. 'So, I just started working it out. And I got there just before they took everyone in. So, I wasn't there when they did it. John sensed it. I'd warned him, but he sensed it, and he got Ian and him out before they got everybody together. The supply boat came, and we took it over. And then we radioed in. John messaged the fisheries protection vessel. We called everybody we could. We set off the Epirb, DSC, gave an SOS. And you guys came.'

'Paul's very lucky,' said Macleod.

'Well, you've got him. He's not that lucky,' said Hope.

'He's very lucky,' said Macleod again. 'If Clarissa were here, she'd have killed him. He would have killed your baby. She would have killed him.' Hope stared at Macleod and she knew he wasn't joking. 'The military guys couldn't have stopped her.'

'Are we flying away then?' said Hope.

'There's a vessel on its way. It'll take everyone into custody. The military will deal with it. Then we'll have to look at what this is. Do they take this as terrorism? Do the police handle it? Who's in charge? At the moment, that's all that's being spoken about. We're just, well, glad it's over. How many went down in the pods?'

'Seven,' said Hope. 'I think it's seven.'

'So seven dead?'

'Eight,' said Hope. 'Eight dead, and I think there might be another one, but you won't find the body.'

'Why?' asked Macleod.

'I have papers saying that the boss was out of control. I didn't quite understand what they meant, but I do now. Somebody stashed them, hid them in my pod, and I think that person is dead because if they got off here, they'd have warned somebody. I think they might be down in the sea. When do you want my statement?' said Hope.

'Don't worry about statements,' said Macleod. 'You, John, and Ian are going to be flown back. We're going to a military base initially, but you'll get all the treatment and everything else. I'll be there in a bit. We need to clear up here, work out what we have to do. Jona might be coming over as well. I just need to talk to people about jurisdiction and the rest of it. We also need to keep the press away from here.'

Hope turned and looked at John. She walked over, and as he stood up, she held him tight. 'We're going home,' she said.

'We're going home.'

'Yes,' he said.

Hope reached into the baby carrier and took out her little one. She wrapped her arms around him and looked over at Seoras. Macleod stared back, smiling. She then walked with little Ian over to Laura, who was sitting on a seat, crying.

'I can't believe he did this,' she said. 'I thought I knew him. I thought I—'

'Don't beat yourself up,' said Hope. 'He was a pro at it. You were lonely. You were in pain because of what he'd done before, breaking up with you.'

'I was right, though. He was all for the environment. He was all for—'

'Yes, he was all for the environment. But so much so he would kill people,' said Hope. 'We can't be like that, either. But you'll go on. You're not part of this crowd. He just brought you in. Alison Mathers will have questions to answer. Paul will. Hamish and the rest of them. I don't know how it will go, but you'll be taken away from here soon. I know you're innocent of anything. You're just a victim, like me.'

'Why did you not say you were a detective at the start to everyone?'

'People don't act the same when you say you're a detective. They become suspicious of you, wanting to know what you're looking for from them. You have to maintain the distance, but I'm glad you survived. You're a decent person. Go find a decent man. And if they offer you help, take all of it.'

She turned and saw Macleod talking to John. Coming back over, she saw John look at her.

'He says they'll sort it out. Might have to be an inquiry as to what happened.'

'You saved Hope's life,' said Macleod. 'I will not tell you it's easy to live with the death of someone, but you did it because they were going to kill her. You did the right thing. Acted, saved a life. You saved the mother of your child. You saved our Hope. I will get you all the help I can. This will not be you for the rest of your life. This will not be something that you can't live with. You will learn to live with it. You will learn to be at some sort of peace again.'

Hope took John in her arms, and the three of them went to walk off. As she did so, Paul stood up, his hands behind his back, spooking the guards slightly.

'When I get out of here, I'll look you up.'

Hope cast him a look and then went to walk off. From the corner of her eyes, she saw Macleod storming over. The old man was never the sleekest, but she swore the next five steps he took were done with a force that came from deep inside. Macleod stepped up in front of Paul and hit him straight to the teeth with the hardest punch she'd ever seen Macleod deliver. Paul fell backwards, his nose bloody, spitting out globules of blood.

'The only reason you're still breathing,' said Macleod, 'is that my godson survived.'

'Did you see what he did to me?' cried Paul.

'I saw the inspector come over. I saw you take a shot at him, trying to headbutt him. Inspector moved out of the way. You smashed your face on this vase here,' said a soldier, picking it up. He then dropped the vase on the floor. 'Vase fell and smashed. We restrained the prisoner. I believe your helicopter will be here soon. I think you're very lucky, because the inspector caught you and set you back down in the chair gently.'

'That's exactly what I saw too, Captain,' said another soldier. Paul swore. But Macleod simply nodded his head to the two soldiers. He walked away. And Hope stopped him.

'You didn't need to do that. That wasn't you.'

'It's why I'm retiring, Hope. You can't be that person forever. Trust me, I'm doing everything I can not to kill that guy at the moment. You get older, you change. The fuses shorten. Everything becomes harder. You become more agitated. You find it difficult to stay in control. That's why I'm leaving it to you.'

He raised his fist, holding it up between her and him. 'And that also hurts so bad,' he said. She could watch him flexing his hand, clearly in pain. 'He deserved that,' said Macleod. 'He deserved it. I'll see you shortly. Go get your helicopter.'

They went to the military helicopter and were strapped in. Hope let John hold on to Ian because he seemed to need him. She put her arms around both her boys. As the helicopter lifted, she looked down at the dream she had. It was to be a wonderful holiday, a send-off, a time for the pair of them, for all three of them to be together. All she wanted to do now was never see that structure again.

Read on to discover the Patrick
Smythe series!

THE
WOMAN ON
THE MARINA
A PATRICK SMYTHE
MYSTERY THRILLER
G R JORDAN

Patrick Smythe is a former Northern Irish policeman who after suffering an amputation after a bomb blast, takes to the sea between the west coast of Scotland and his homeland to ply his trade as a private investigator. Join Paddy as he tries to work to his own ethics while knowing how to bend the rules he once enforced. Working from his beloved motorboat 'Craigantlet', Paddy decides to rescue a drug mule in this short story from the pen of G R Jordan.

Join G R Jordan's monthly newsletter about forthcoming releases and special writings for his tribe of avid readers and then receive your free Patrick Smythe short story.

Go to https://bit.ly/PatrickSmythe for your Patrick Smythe journey to start.

About the Author

GR Jordan is a self-published author who finally decided at forty that in order to have an enjoyable lifestyle, his creative beast within would have to be unleashed. His books mirror that conflict in life where acts of decency contend with self-promotion, goodness stares in horror at evil, and kindness blindsides us when we at our worst. Corrupting our world with his parade of wondrous and horrific characters, he highlights everyday tensions with fresh eyes whilst taking his methodical, intelligent mainstays on a roller-coaster ride of dilemmas, all the while suffering the banter of their provocative sidekicks.

A graduate of Loughborough University where he masqueraded as a chemical engineer but ultimately played American football, Gary had worked at changing the shape of cereal flakes and pulled a pallet truck for a living. Watching vegetables freeze at -40'C was another career highlight and he was also one of the Scottish Highlands "blind" air traffic controllers.

These days he has graduated to answering a telephone to people in trouble before telephoning other people to sort it out.

Having flirted with most places in the UK, he is now based in the Isle of Lewis in Scotland where his free time is spent between raising a young family with his wife, writing, figuring out how to work a loom and caring for a small flock of chickens. Luckily, his writing is influenced by his varied work and life experience as the chickens have not been the poetical inspiration he had hoped for!

You can connect with me on:
🌐 https://www.grjordan.com
f https://facebook.com/carpetlessleprechaun

Subscribe to my newsletter:
✉ https://bit.ly/PatrickSmythe

Also by G R Jordan

G R Jordan writes across multiple genres including crime, dark and action adventure fantasy, feel good fantasy, mystery thriller and horror fantasy. Below is a selection of his work. Whilst all books are available across online stores, signed copies are available at his personal shop.

Exit Stage Right (Highlands & Islands Detective Thrillers #50)

https://grjordan.com/product/exit-stage-right

The largest theatre production in Inverness history. A deadly shooting of the show's star in the final act. Can Macleod rise above the showbiz rumour and bitterness to find the killer in the troupe?

Attending the largest production in Inverness theatre history, DCI Macleod is called into action as the star of the show is shot dead before the stunned audience. When what looks like a tragic accident is shown to be otherwise, the team start to delve into the embittered history and reckless finances of the production. In the public cauldron where accusation and denial seems to be a daily fix for the public, Seoras Macleod must one last time hunt down a killer. But when everyone's an actor of the highest quality, how do you know what's real and what's a performance?

Will Macleod be allowed one last hurrah?

Kirsten Stewart Thrillers

https://grjordan.com/product/a-shot-at-democracy

Join Kirsten Stewart on a shadowy ride through the underbelly of the Highlands of Scotland where among the beauty and splendour of the majestic landscape lies corruption and intrigue to match any city. From murders to extortion, missing children to criminals operating above the law, the Highland former detective must learn a tougher edge to her work as she puts her own life on the line to protect those who cannot defend themselves.

Having left her beloved murder investigation team far behind, Kirsten has to battle personal tragedy and loss while adapting to a whole new way of executing her duties where your mistakes are your own. As Kirsten comes to terms with working with the new team, she often operates as the groups solo field agent, placing herself in danger and trouble to rescue those caught on the dark side of life. With action packed scenes and tense scenarios of murder and greed, the Kirsten Stewart thrillers will have you turning page after page to see your favourite Scottish lass home!

There's life after Macleod, but a whole new world of death!

Jac's Revenge (A Jac Moonshine Thriller #1)

https://grjordan.com/product/jacs-revenge

An unexpected hit makes Debbie a widow. The attention of her man's killer spawns a brutal yet classy alter ego. But how far can you play the game before it takes over your life?

All her life, Debbie Parlor lived in her man's shadow, knowing his work was never truly honest. She turned her head from news stories and rumours. But when he was disposed of for his smile to placate a rival crime lord, Jac Moonshine was born. And when Debbie is paid compensation for her loss like her car was written off, Jac decides that enough is enough.

Get on board with this tongue-in-cheek revenge thriller that will make you question how far you would go to avenge a loved one, and how much you would enjoy it!

A Giant Killing (Siobhan Duffy Mysteries #1)

https://grjordan.com/product/a-giant-killing

A body lies on the Giant's boot. Discord, as the master of secrets has been found. Can former spy Siobhan Duffy find the killer before they execute her former colleagues?

When retired operative Siobhan Duffy sees the killing of her former master in the paper, her unease sends her down a path of discovery and fear. Aided by her young housekeeper and scruff of a gardener, Siobhan begins a quest to discover the reason for her spy boss' death and unravels a can of worms today's masters would rather keep closed. But in a world of secrets, the difference between revenge and simple, if brutal, housekeeping becomes the hardest truth to know.

The past is a child who never leaves home!

9 781917 497374